No One Said It'd Be Easy

Where ever I go

Suzeth Mawote

authorHOUSE®

AuthorHouse™ UK Ltd.
500 Avebury Boulevard
Central Milton Keynes, MK9 2BE
www.authorhouse.co.uk
Phone: 08001974150

First published by AuthorHouse 3/2/2011

ISBN: 978-1-4520-9329-1 (sc)

This book is printed on acid-free paper.

To my family,

The reason of my existence,

May God always bless us...

And to someone very special (Isidro Queta),

Also a special thanks to Luis Margarido, Victoria Ekpenyong, Chinwe and Gbenga Akintan for all the support.

With all my heart and Love,

Suzeth Mawote.

I

The Farewell

That Saturday in September was an unforgettable day for the whole family. At six in the morning they were all wide awake, with the exception of Hadjame, who was in the habit of getting up only when she smelt breakfast or heard her mother shouting. 'Dona Mónica', as her mother was known, was giving instructions to her maid Maria from the kitchen. Lying in her bed, Hadjame listened to the music that filtered through the thin wall between her room and that of her thirteen-year-old sister, Chimene. Her mind wandered far and wide, beyond the white ceiling of her room.

'I know I'll love you. All my life, I'll love you,' Hadjame sang a song her best friend Xissola, or 'Xi', had dedicated to her. They went to the same school, and always shared their fears and their secrets—secrets that troubled her older brother Kizua, especially when the subject was boys. 'Sibling jealousy' her mother always said. Luckily Kizua, now eighteen, was away studying medicine in England. At fifteen, but well-developed, Hadjame already seemed like a full-grown woman, if rather shy. But seventeen-year-old Xissola, with her outgoing nature, was a perfect balance to her friend. Naturally blessed with dark complexions and curly hair, both were highly intelligent and people often misjudged their age; they were often taken for older than they were. Some even called them 'precocious', but not their real friends and family. Perhaps this was why Hadjame's parents gave her the freedom to be away from their protection at so young an age.

'Breakfast is on the table,' shouted her mother finally. 'And there's orange cake,' she added for emphasis. Chimene jumped out of bed and ran into the kitchen, picking up a knife as if ready for action. She was brought up short by her mother, who slapped her hand and took the knife from her. She sent Chimene off to wash first and to call her older sister. Annoyed, Chimene stuck out her lip and called her sister by hammering on her door. Then she ran off to the bathroom to wash.

'Coming,' Hadjame replied in a sad voice. She was a born dreamer, and for her, her room was the best part of the house. Her bags packed, and lying on her bed, Hadjame imagined what life would be like far away from her mother's arms, her grandmother's affection, her sister's sulks, her brother's jealousy, Maria's food, secrets shared with Xissola, and the wisdom of Doctor André Kaquengue, her father, who was sitting on the veranda with his glasses on his nose, buried in his newspaper, pretending to read. Although inside the whole family was anxious, outside the same old music was playing: the noise of cars on the motorway, the slamming of doors in other apartments, and the upstairs neighbour, who seemed to drag his furniture about every morning. But this was what life in a city as big as Luanda was all about; rushing about was synonymous with modernity.

'Hello! Grandma, how are you?' Hadjame answered her phone, which sat close to the head of her bed, and she lay back down again to continue her conversation.

'Little Hadjame!' said her grandmother affectionately. 'I'm feeling much better, thank God, though I'm still sleepy, because of the sedatives,' she continued in a frail voice.

'You have to get plenty of rest, Grandma', said Hadjame.

Her grandma suffered from high blood pressure, and the whole family tried very hard to keep her cheerful and avoid strong emotions. Kizua especially, with his witty jokes, knew how to cheer her up. Perhaps that was why he was her favourite grandchild, or perhaps it was because he was the only boy. 'He is my man,' boasted Grandma Madalena, who'd been a widow for over twenty years. Kizua's departure for England troubled her greatly. She said that she might die without ever seeing her grandson again. 'Lots of those who cross the seas get so caught up in what they see, they never come back,' she would complain. And now it was Hadjame's turn to leave. At least she was not crossing the sea, only land, going away from the city.

'You don't sound very happy,' said Grandma, picking up a touch of despondency in her granddaughter's voice.

'I'm fine, Grandma,' Hadjame said, trying to brighten up. She would really have liked to open her heart, but she didn't want to burden her grandmother with her own worries, so she held back her tears and changed the subject. 'What I'm really going to miss is your cooking.' Hadjame sometimes wound her mother up, saying that her feijão de óleo de palma[1] was not a patch on Grandma's. 'You don't have to eat them,' her mother would point out, to everyone's amusement.

'You'll have plenty of opportunities to eat my cooking when you come back. Have a good journey, my love, and God bless you!'

'Amen,' said Hadjame, agreeing with her in the most formal way, and there were tears in her eyes as she put the phone down. Her mother continued calling for her insistently, and Chimene decided to come and get her again.

'Hey sleepyhead, wake up slacker, and don't even think about wearing the yellow blouse, know what ah mean?' Chimene's slangy speech was influenced by her schoolfriends and the Brazilian soap operas she watched. It made her seem like she had totally different parents from those who'd raised Hadjame and Kizua, both of whom were more correct in their speech.

'The blouse is in the chest of drawers, babe, but hey, get off my case, it's still early,' replied Hadjame, imitating her sister's tone. She smiled because it felt a bit ridiculous. 'Impoverished language', her father would call it.

---

1 Traditional Angolan recipe (beans, onions and garlic with palm oil)

'Hey, you're a quick learner!' said Chimene, pleased. 'You should go away more often. Maybe then you could leave me your entire wardrobe.' Chimene grabbed the blouse and leapt out of the room, just escaping the pillow hurled by her sister. She always preferred her older sister's clothes, even if they didn't suit her, and they fought a lot over this, causing their mother to intervene. Keen to see how the new blouse would look on her, Chimene ran to her mirror, and then came back to show her sister, posing like a model with her hand on her waist, to see what she thought.

'I'm already regretting letting you have it,' teased Hadjame. 'It looks good on you, but in return, will you play my tune again, please?' asked Hadjame, putting her hands together in a pleading gesture.

'Today I'll do anything for you, but don't get used to it,' said Chimene. 'And stop daydreaming,' she added, hurling back her sister's pillow as she withdrew.

'Thanks, little sister,' shouted Hadjame when she heard the music coming from her room. 'I know I'll love you…', she sang along with it.

'Hadjaaame!' Her father interrupted her singing in a stern and authoritarian voice. 'Didn't you hear your mother calling?' he shouted from the veranda. Almost falling out of bed in fright, Hadjame got up immediately.

'I'm finishing packing my bags, Dad,' she lied. Before going to wash up, she decided first to open the window, and the rays of sunshine filled her room with intense light, which almost dazzling her. Hadjame watched the pedestrians scurrying along the waterfront, the infernal traffic on the potholed roads, the news vendors running hither and thither, and the fish sellers carrying their tubs of fish under the burning sun. All over Luanda, it was total bustle. Finally she looked towards the horizon of the blue sea, which, from her window on the seventh floor, offered a beautiful panorama. With the breeze on her face, she closed her eyes and drifted in the peace of her own thoughts. She associated the summer sun and Saturdays with calalú stew,[2] with all the family gathered in Grandma Madalena's garden in Marçal, with dance music playing—Kizomba, Kuduro, and Semba.[3] They would dance and laugh at Kizua's jokes until the early hours. Alternatively they would take a boat trip, to the paradise island of Mussulo where they sunbathed on the beautiful crystalline sandy beaches, dived into the blue waters, and sat together on the esplanade, only returning home late on Sunday. 'An almost perfect, perhaps a perfect paradise,' she murmured to herself, coming back to reality with a sigh.

'Decided to show up at long last, dcaric?' hcr sistcr said rudely when Hadjame joined them at the table. Their father automatically chided Chimene.

'I'll not have that kind of language in my house,' he said. Chimene was amused by her father's anger, while Hadjame was scared to death. More like her father physically, Chimene was the reflection that their father often preferred not to see.

2 An Angolan stew made with spinach-like leaves and dried meat.

3 Traditional Angolan dances

'André, please, let's not start the day with an argument,' said their mother, trying to smooth things over. Her mother was always the calm one, attending to her children's needs, compared to her father, who claimed he had a lot of work in his consulting room. He worked nights and extra hours at any time of day in cases of emergency. They were both happy, though. Perhaps when her mother married a doctor she was already aware of these demands on his time, but Hadjame could never understand how she could be happy, not being able to work, at her husband's request.

'Sorry I'm late,' said Hadjame, ignoring her sister's comment and pulling out a chair. She sat at the kitchen table, where they always had breakfast together. The maid poured orange juice into her glass, and Hadjame smiled at her in thanks. Maria had been there at the birth of all three children, so she knew what they liked best, perhaps better than their mother did. She was a strong woman in spite of her advancing age, and she was by now part of the family.

When everyone was seated, Dona Mónica asked her husband to say grace. It was their custom to say grace before meals. They all accompanied Doctor André silently. A few minutes later, Xissola arrived to say goodbye to her friend, and they invited her to join them. Because of her close friendship with Hadjame, Xissola was always welcome. After breakfast, several other friends and neighbours called in to wish Hadjame well; many brought presents. She was very touched, and although she had promised not to cry that day, there were tears in her eyes.

'Don't take too long,' her father warned her, as he went down to the garage under the building with the car keys in his hand. Hadjame thanked her friends and said goodbye to them. Then she opened Xissola's present. She let out a small 'ooh' when she saw the silver, heart-shaped pendant. Inside, Xissola had put both their photos, one in each side.

'Oh Xi, it's lovely! Thank you.' They hugged each other.

'So that you'll always remember me. I'm going to really miss you,' said Xissola with a sad voice.

'I'll wear it always, right next to my heart.' The two girls hugged each other again. As Xissola helped her put the necklace on, Chimene came out of her room carrying a gift for her sister. Hadjame smiled when she saw the expression on her face, with a look that said 'I don't know why I'm giving it to you, but I suppose you deserve it'.

'For you,' said Chimene abruptly. Hadjame didn't believe her sister had just given her her favourite CD. 'I'm really going to miss you,' Chimene admitted. Two years younger than Hadjame, Chimene found it difficult to express her feelings, and they hugged each other tenderly. Not wishing to be left out, her mother handed Hadjame a Bible.

'I know, Mum,' said Hadjame. 'Put it by the bed, and read a psalm every night, before I go to sleep.'

'I hope it becomes music to your ears,' murmured her mother. The three girls laughed, and Hadjame kissed her mother on the cheek. Then Hadjame said goodbye to Maria, who was dragging her bags down the stairs, crying at seeing her leave. The four of them went out to look for her father. On the fourth floor, Hadjame suddenly stopped.

'I've left something in the house!' she said.

'Don't be long. Dad's already been waiting a long time,' her mother reminded her. Hadjame nodded and ran back up to the seventh floor. Back within the four walls of the place where she had been born and grown up, Hadjame looked all around, as if she were saying goodbye forever. Then she took refuge in her room and sat down on her bed with a pensive air. She picked up her teddy bear, a present Xissola had gotten her from the fairgrounds, and hugged it to her chest, realising how far away she would be from her friends and family, until the sound of banging on the door woke her from her reverie. Maria told her that her father said to hurry up. Hadjame pulled herself together and, saying goodbye to Maria again, she hurried down to her family, who were waiting in silence for her in the car.

'Are you trying to put off leaving again?' her father asked her impatiently. Hadjame had already postponed her journey the previous week, saying it was too early. 'The real moment of departure,' she thought. There was no alternative. She apologised meekly and sat down on the back seat beside her sister and friend.

'Were you crying?' Xissola whispered in her ear. Hadjame nodded. They could both read each other's thoughts, so in order not to give herself away Hadjame quickly turned to look out of the window, and wave goodbye to some neighbours. Silence fell over the car as they went along until, screwing up her courage, she cleared the lump in her throat and spoke up at last.

'I can't believe that I'm going to be away from you for three years,' she wailed. Hadjame felt her adolescence being forcibly taken from her. Her parents consoled her, telling her that the time would pass quickly, and that they could always be together for the holidays.

'The province of Kwanza-Sul isn't very far from Luanda,' said her father. 'And you won't be the only one in this situation; it's one of the best schools in the country. Lots manage, and you will manage too.'

'I've heard that the new pupils get mistreated by the older ones,' said Chimene, to scare her. Xissola nudged her with her elbow. Hadjame was upset by her sister's unnecessary comments, even if they were true.

'You are unbelievable! Even with your sister going away, you can't manage to try and cheer her up?' scolded her father. Feeling hurt, Chimene said she was sorry, and Hadjame knew that deep down she was only teasing. Hadjame looked at her sister, to comfort her, and she retorted by sticking her tongue out, opening her eyes wide and pulling faces. Hadjame barely smiled. A bit on the sensitive side, Hadjame sometimes wished she was more like her sister. Chimene had a different way of expressing her feelings.

'As I was saying,' continued her father, 'you must always remember what I've told you…'

'No one said it'd be easy,' chorused the two sisters, familiar with the maxim, and they all laughed, including their father. Through the window of the car they could already see the bustle at the bus station: passengers on their way to the four corners of the country, street vendors earning their daily bread, as Grandma Madalena used to say. When they passed a young man actually selling bread, Hadjame remembered Kizua's joke. 'But Grandma, how can he be selling bread and earning bread at the same time?' And Grandmother had chased him with a slipper in her hand. Street selling was illegal and the vendors moved about cautiously, keeping an eye out for the civil police. All the commotion stirred up the red earth that had been dried by the sun, raising a cloud of dust, so no one could go through the place and keep clean.

'So much chaos in this place!' exclaimed Chimene, and her sister and her friend agreed. Their mother was amused by the panic on their faces, and she frightened them further by saying there were thieves about. The three girls could not believe that they would have to deal with such a thing as they carried the bags to the bus. Hadjame was clutching onto her mother's arm when suddenly, amid all the confusion, someone snatched the necklace from her neck.

'Help, help! My necklace,' cried Hadjame, terrified. The police took no notice, so her mother ran after the thief. Seeing he was pursued, and without much possibility of escape, he threw the necklace to the ground and disappeared into the crowd. Breathless, her mother picked up the necklace and gave it back to her daughter, who put it in her bag, feeling really scared.

'You could enter a marathon, Mum,' said Chimene.

'When I married your mother, I knew that I'd be safe with her, even from thieves,' put in her father as soon as they told him what had happened, and they all laughed uncontrollably, except their mother.

'What would become of you, if it wasn't for me?' said Mónica, stoutly. 'Come on. Don't make me have to run again.' She pulled her daughter. And unable to contain herself any longer, she, too, began to laugh, until her ribs hurt.

'This is what I'm going to miss,' said Hadjame, feeling sad. Holding back the tears that were giving her away, she said goodbye to her father, sister and her friend, and climbed with her mother onto the bus which was due to leave at 10:30 AM. Her sister stood sobbing in Xissola's arms. Xissola consoled her as they waved goodbye, until the bus disappeared down the road.

2

The Welcome

There was a shortage of transport to the provinces. Because of the current civil war, drivers were increasingly unwilling to risk their lives taking that journey. The few who were prepared to do so always travelled fully laden with passengers and goods, including chickens and ducks. Inside the bus the smell was unbearable, while from the window a strong wind mixed with sand and dust beat hard against Hadjame's face. She was amazed by everything she saw: burnt-out, abandoned cars; clothing scattered on the grass; signs warning about mines—all the legacy of the war. With the music turned up loud, the driver put his foot down hard as he traversed the potholed roads.

'Please go slowly, comrade driver,' shouted several frightened passengers. The calmer ones, like Hadjame's mother, perhaps to make her feel more secure, prayed at every jolt. Others told stories of enemy attacks on those roads, leading some people to fall asleep, or to pretend they were asleep. 'Please turn down the music, comrade driver,' other passengers shouted. But the music was a distraction, to deal with the fear and help the driver's concentration. All this was quite new for Hadjame. In contrast, there was lovely countryside, marshes, rivers, and forests with birds singing. She saw monkeys jumping from tree to tree, playing, while a sloth stayed unmoving on its branch. The whole scene was extraordinarily beautiful.

'How much longer till we get there, Mum?' Hadjame asked her mother for the third time and got the same answer she'd gotten each time: 'Not long now, love.' For Hadjame this 'not long' seemed to last forever. As they neared their destination, at the top of the sunny mountains, they came to a small village where semi-naked children ran along beside the bus with smiles on their faces. The adults working in the fields seemed happy, cultivating their small plantations of maize and cassava under the burning sun. Their houses were very small and built of scrub grass with zinc roofs shining in the sunlight. Feeling compassionate towards it all and storing in her mind what she saw, Hadjame felt her eyes fill with tears. The other passengers looked at her, astonished, and laughed at her innocence.

'Don't be alarmed, my dear. These people sometimes end up a lot happier than we are in the big city,' her mother said to reassure her.

'I swear I wouldn't survive a day here, with no running water, no electricity, and no basic sanitation. How do they survive like this?' Hadjame said, wiping her tears. Her mother didn't know what else to say to her.

'Look! Do you see those buildings in the distance?' Dona Mónica said to distract her. 'That's where we're going.' It was 6:30 PM and the sun was already going down when they finally arrived at their destination. The town appeared to be asleep, with hardly any traffic compared to the big city. The only movement came from the small market on one side and from a few kupapatas.[4]

'Eight hours' journey,' her mother calculated. 'Welcome to Sumbe,' she said to her daughter.

'Aaargh! I can't feel my legs,' complained Hadjame. She'd been sitting for such a long time she had to bang her foot on the ground to revive it. 'Are we going by motorbike?' she asked as soon as they had pulled her bags from the bus, anxious for the new experience.

'Your boarding school is very near, my dear. We can walk,' said her mother.

'You thought eight hours was near, Mum,' her daughter reminded her, and they both laughed. Dragging her bags, they made their way to the boarding school where Hadjame was to stay for the next three years. As they drew near to the school, they could see various people milling about. Old pupils and new pupils accompanied by their parents like her were arriving in droves.

'Another little Mummy's girl', mocked the old, 'veteran' students, when they saw her arriving clinging onto her mother. Embarrassed, Hadjame moved away from her mother slightly.

'Pay no attention to their insults,' her mother said,

---

4 Motorcyclists who act as taxi drivers.

urging her on. They headed for the headmaster's office, where they were met by a man with a rather stern voice, who reminded her of her father. It was the headmaster himself, 'Director Kalunga,' who was courteously greeting all the new students. They introduced themselves, and the headmaster filled them in about what would happen next.

'You don't seem very happy,' he said to Hadjame.

'She's a bit alarmed by the bustle,' her mother explained.

'Oh dear! Don't worry, my child. You will be in good hands. It won't be long before you have lots of friends. There will be five girls in your room with you.' Hadjame could not believe what she had just heard.

'Five girls?' she exclaimed. 'Couldn't I have a room of my own?' she suggested timidly. She was used to the privacy of her own room, where even Chimene had to ask before coming in.

'Unfortunately not,' said the headmaster.

'Or I could go and stay somewhere else,' said Hadjame, hoping to see light at the end of the tunnel.

'Certainly not,' interrupted her mother. Hadjame threw her a beseeching look. Anything would be better than sharing a room with five other girls, and living away from her mother among these horrible girls. 'You're only fifteen,' her mother reminded her. Once again her age seemed to get in the way. Sometimes she wished she was eighteen, but that day seemed a long way off.

'In that case, you will have to stay in the residence, for safety reasons,' concluded the headmaster. Defeated by the two of them, Hadjame set off with them to look around the residence. The headmaster showed them all around. They followed his gesticulations with their eyes, and when he was pointing towards the boys' dormitories, a boy, stark naked, barely covering his front with his hands, ran from the 'dibuka,' or bathhouse, to his room.

'My goodness, what on earth was that?' asked Dona Mónica, shocked. Hadjame laughed at the scene and her mother turned her away.

'A disobedient pupil,' intoned the head. 'No one is allowed into the area of the opposite sex,' he explained calmly. In a very old, brown two-storey building, the boys were on the left and the girls on the right of a long corridor with several dormitories off it. A small space in the middle led to the stairs. That was where the imaginary boundary began.

'Hey, pretty little new girl, what's your name?' yelled one of the old boys, standing at the end of his corridor. Unfortunately, Hadjame couldn't turn around, prevented by her mother.

'Leave the girl in peace, Bonitão,' rebuked the head. Only after the head's reassurance did her mother let go of Hadjame.

'I can see that you're enjoying this situation,' chided her mother. Hadjame smiled at the boy's name, 'Bonitão', which rather matched his good looks. Apologising to her mother, Hadjame tried to suppress her laughter. Her mother threw her a warning look, and they said goodbye to the head, who was not allowed to enter the girl's side of the building. Pulled by her arm, Hadjame followed her mother in silence, and then they both burst out laughing.

'I'm still thinking twice about leaving you in this place,' said her mother. Laughing, they went into the dormitory. There Hadjame was reunited with her ex-schoolfriend Marta, whom she hadn't seen for over five years. Marta's family was always travelling because her father was a diplomat. The two girls hugged each other with relief. Dona Mónica greeted Hadjame's old friend warmly, pleased that her daughter already had someone to keep her company.

'Are you the only one here? When did you arrive?' asked Hadjame.

'I got here a week ago. I was the first to arrive,' she explained excitedly, and the two girls began to chat about their courses. Marta was studying architecture, while Hadjame was planning to concentrate on social sciences, and then train in psychology.

'Marta! Ooooh, Martaaaa! I'm hungry,' shouted Bonitão in the middle of the corridor. Hadjame and her mother recognised his voice, but they looked puzzled, not understanding what he meant.

'The old boys are always asking for our snacks,' Marta explained. She looked a little embarrassed, but she went off to see him with a smile on her face. An extrovert and rather attractive, Marta seemed to have got used to the new surroundings very quickly.

'Seems rather well known, this Bonitão,' exclaimed Hadjame.

'I don't want you associating with people like that,' her mother warned her, and she nodded.

'Can I spend the night in the hotel with you?' Hadjame said, tactically changing the subject. Her mother understood; she could see that Hadjame felt uneasy in this place.

'Only if you don't forget that I'm going home the day after tomorrow.'

'I know, Mum. You don't need to remind me,' murmured Hadjame. And they left for the hotel hand in hand. Hadjame spent the next two nights there with her mother.

3
Anarchy

The following Monday, Hadjame felt she was being abandoned to the herd when her mother returned with her to the students' residence. From now on, she would have no member of her family near to her. It would be just her and God, as her mother put it. Bonitão popped up on his way to breakfast in the canteen, which was in an annexe behind the residence building. He shouted out her name in the form of a song, drawing everyone's attention to her. Hadjame smiled awkwardly.

'Bonitão, this is my daughter. Please take good care of her,' intervened her mother, noting his popularity.

'Don't worry, auntie, I'll look after her as though she were my niece,' he replied with a smile. He came up and greeted them both courteously.

'How do you know my name?' asked Hadjame, curious. 'Oh, I know! Marta told you,' she said, suddenly realising. She relaxed and they chatted with him for a while about student life in the residence. Hadjame was feeling lost, but Bonitão told her he would be her protector. And although he was a bit of a joker, he was well respected by everyone. Late for breakfast, and at risk of finding the door shut, which was open in which case he would have to go without, Bonitão said goodbye and ran off quickly to the canteen. Luckily Hadjame had already had her breakfast at the hotel, and didn't have to subject herself to yet another trial so soon. In the dormitory, two other new girls had arrived the night before. Only the two old girls had not yet arrived to make up the full complement, and from what Bonitão had said, they would make the new girls' lives hell on earth. Hadjame introduced herself, but only Francisca replied. Cláudia was wrapped up in her sheets, crying.

'Apparently she didn't want to come here to study, but her parents made her. She didn't even go for breakfast today,' whispered Marta. Hadjame nodded to her mother, suggesting she go over to console her. But although she stopped crying, Cláudia lay back down on her bed, turned her face to the wall, and covered herself up again with her sheet. Hadjame's mother shrugged her shoulders, indifferently. Dona Mónica stayed with the girls for some hours, leaving them with a cascade of advice. At 11 AM, with no more time to lose, she said goodbye to them all. She kissed the top of her daughter's head and left. Hadjame was consoled by her new friends.

'Cheer up, it's nearly midday. There's grilled pork with fried potatoes for lunch,' said Marta excitedly. She licked her lips, as though the meal was already in front of her.

'And supper is at six,' added Francisca.

'That's when I used to have lunch, when I got home late,' joked Hadjame, feeling in slightly better spirits. And they all smiled. In their attempt to get there first, and not miss the chance to sample the 'grilled pork with fried potatoes' by getting there too late, the four girls, carrying their own cutlery as was required, were already at the canteen door at midday precisely. At the head of the queue was Bonitão, with another young man beside him, both standing in the doorway. They were only allowing the new students of their choice to go in. The old ones themselves went in anyhow, taking no notice of the order in which they arrived. Hadjame was rather shocked by this anarchic behaviour.

'We'll all get in soon,' Marta reassured her. Used to the scenario, Marta was more interested in looking at the good-looking boys who were going in, especially the 'nice-looking young man', as she referred to the boy at Bonitão's side. He was whispering in Bonitão's ear; it was obvious that they both were talking about the new girls. The three girls whispered together, and laughed easily now and then, but Hadjame decided to give up in the face of such humiliation.

'I'm leaving!' she said, moving away annoyed. Suddenly she heard someone calling her name and she turned around to see who it was.

'You, Hadjame', said Bonitão. 'You can go in now.' But her shyness kept her standing where she was. 'Probably the one causing the whole situation,' she thought angrily. When her eyes met those of the young man standing beside Bonitão, he smiled at her and ushered her in. All eyes turned on her then, and Hadjame wanted the ground to swallow her up.

'Go on, Hadjame. Go on in,' her friends pushed her. But she stood like a statue, not moving.

'You can all come in, all four of you,' commanded Bonitão finally, provoking a huge revolt among all those in front of them. But only then did Hadjame manage to move. As though passing along a gangway, beneath the penetrating and silent gaze of the 'nice-looking young man', Hadjame and her friends got in just in time to sample the much longed-for lunch, which contrasted with the general confusion of the place. The canteen was very tumultuous. The old students used mealtimes, something sacred to Hadjame and her family, for their worst behaviour, which made many of the new students give up. As soon as they were served by the cooks, the four girls sat down apprehensively at a far table. Even so, and without any objection, their desserts were taken by some of the old students. They ate as quickly as possible and, to the sound of various insults and whistling, they got away from that place, a place Hadjame could never have imagined existing. On the way out of the canteen someone took her by the arm.

'Hadjame isn't it?' asked the young man, with a friendly smile. Her friends moved away, and waited for her at some distance, whispering.

'How do you know my name?' she asked, startled, trying to break free.

'Bonitão told me,' replied the young man, pleasantly. He let go of her arm and apologised for the embarrassment at the entrance to the canteen. He actually seemed rather contrite.

'Unless you were also part of the anarchy,' she said, disgustedly.

'A little,' he teased her. Furious, Hadjame was about to move off. 'Wait, wait, it wasn't funny, I know. No more jokes,' he went on, while Hadjame looked him up and down seriously. 'Actually, I think I know you from somewhere.' And he was trying to recall the time he had met her. 'I think I remember now,' he said, snapping his fingers. 'I'm Wassi. Don't you remember me?' he asked with a convinced smile. With a relaxed laugh, Hadjame recalled the time she had met him.

'Now I remember. You were Xi's friend. During that unbearable class… You were in love, from what I heard. That's what she told me,' she said enthusiastically, leaving him lost for words.

'Childish pranks. We were just kids,' he said, defensively. 'And how is that crazy girl?'

'She's fine,' replied Hadjame. They chatted for a while about his situation at the boarding school. In his final year, Wassi was studying Mechanics. Marta was gesticulating impatiently from a distance, so she had to hurry.

'Wait, wait!' he asked, and then he picked a flower from the garden at the side of the canteen. 'A flower, for another flower,' he said poetically. Hadjame accepted it and thanked him shyly. They looked at each other in silence for a few seconds. 'Marta's right. He really is a very good-looking young man,' she thought. His penetrating gaze left her mesmerised, and she made an effort to get away.

'What's the hurry? I won't bite,' he joked, spotting her unease. 'Next weekend is the start of the school basketball championships; you can be my guest of honour. You can bring your friends, too,' he said.

'Thank you very much, but I'd better think about it… I've got to go now.' She waved goodbye. Wassi watched her as she ran to meet her friends. Xissola phoned her when she was on her way to meet her friends, and Hadjame told her about meeting up with Wassi. Xissola felt bad at being left behind, because all her old friends were reunited. And suddenly Hadjame was at a loss for words.

'Hello! Hadjame, can you hear me?' asked Xissola. Hadjame was on another planet entirely, staring at the flower she'd been given.

'Xi! I have to hang up,' she said finally. 'The girls have been calling me for ages.'

'Give Marta a kiss from me, and tell her not to steal my friend,' Xissola joked, and the two friends said goodbye. As Hadjame approached her friends, they showered her with questions about Wassi. She told them everything, including the invitation for the following Saturday. Skipping about with happiness, and to the constant whistles of the boys who saw them pass by, they went up to their dormitory.

'Hadjame, Hadjame,' sighed Wassi. Interrogated by Bonitão, who wanted to know what his friend was looking so happy about, Wassi elaborately told him all about Hadjame, and asked him to convince her to go to the pitch. Bonitão looked at him in silence, astonished.

'Don't look at me like that. This time it's serious,' Wassi complained.

'She is pretty, isn't she?' asked Bonitão.

'She's got the loveliest smile I've ever seen,' sighed Wassi.

'I'm not talking about Hadjame; I'm talking about Marta,' Bonitão joked. They both laughed and slapped each other on the back in a gesture of complicity, and Bonitão agreed to help Wassi, because from the look on his friend's face, it really was serious. In the residence, many couples and friends met up in the small space in the middle of the corridor, and stood around chatting until late. Others preferred to sit on the steps, and the more daring crossed over to the other side and slipped surreptitiously into the girls' rooms, especially after supper. There was a kind of check of the rooms carried out by the wardens at the behest of the headmaster's office, but the students always managed to sneak out, hide in the kifato[5] or under the bed. The students on the ground floor sat down on the low walls of the garden

5 A basic wardrobe.

that ran round the residence, and from there they could even hold shouted conversations with those upstairs. It was a kind of freedom that astonished Hadjame, and if she told her parents they would come and fetch her the next day. Here there was neither father nor mother to impose any restrictions. Everything was allowed. The only restriction was set by each person's own conscience. But there was something about this way of life that delighted her. Hadjame knew that one day she would have a story to tell, and when she chatted with Bonitão in the middle of the corridor, he insisted she go to the pitch with them.

'But you still have five days to think it over. If not, I'll complain to your mother, because you've been disobedient to your uncle,' he teased.

'I might very well change my mind.' Hadjame joined in her friend's joke. Then they said goodbye, and Hadjame went back to her room. The other three girls had already all gone to bed. Lying in her bed, her thoughts turned to Wassi. Smiling, she put the flower under her pillow and fell asleep. In a few days with her pretty face, enchanting smile, clear brown eyes, and curly hair, Hadjame had all the young men in the residence vying for her attention. Time seemed to fly Saturday was already here and Hadjame would definitely not go to the sportsground. She thought it would only give rise to a lot of gossip and she didn't want to be surrounded by mocking old girls. So she convinced her friends not to go. When he learned of her decision, after the basketball match, Wassi thought her attitude was ridiculous, but he had to respect it. Hadjame seemed to be a very conservative girl who didn't like drawing attention to herself.

'An awkward girl,' he sighed, 'but I'll have all the patience in the world.'

'Best of luck, mate,' laughed Bonitão. Tapping him on the chest, he congratulated him on his win. Within a few hours, Bonitão had spread it around the whole residence that Wassi was in love with Hadjame. Furious, Hadjame told her friend off, and he apologised in front of Wassi as they chatted in the middle of the corridor that evening. It was too late; her name, in a way she least wanted, was on everyone's lips. Wassi, too, tried to calm her down, saying it was only a joke, and she ended up angry with both of them, reminding them that this was precisely why she hadn't gone to the sportsfield to watch him.

'You're still lovely even when you're upset, did you realise?' Wassi said to tease her. Without giving him time to apologise, Hadjame went off to her room, visibly annoyed with the two friends. 'Aren't you at least going to congratulate me for winning?' Wassi called after her.

'What's eating you?' asked Marta as Hadjame slammed the door so as not to hear Wassi and Bonitão, who had followed her almost to the door, trying to apologise. Marta came to the conclusion that it was the main news, so she decided not to ask any more questions, and the other two girls followed suit.

'Can I turn out the light?' Hadjame asked in a miserable voice.

'Noooo!' chorused Francisca and Marta. The three of

them always argued before going to sleep, so Cláudia suggested that Francisca and Marta should go to sleep first; then she or Hadjame could turn the light out later. They all agreed. It was very difficult for Hadjame to adapt to being surrounded by people with different habits and cultures. She felt lost when she remembered Bonitão's gossip-mongering and she really missed her family. She wept quietly and in secret in her bed.

'Have you heard that the old girls from the other rooms are already making the new girls' lives hell?' Marta asked them. Cláudia was scared to death, just thinking about what it was going to be like when the old girls of their room arrived. Hadjame butted in to say that she would have to get up early the next day, because she was going to church.

'Goodnight,' they all said. In the early hours of the morning, when all three were asleep, Hadjame got up and turned out the light. She went back to bed and tried to sleep, but was startled by loud banging on the door. They all woke up, terrified. Cláudia jumped out of her bed and ran into Francisca's which was underneath her bunk.

'Shhhhhhhh, don't turn on the light,' whispered Hadjame.

'Wake up, new girls, wake up. This is no time to be sleeping. You haven't seen anything yet. It was worse in our time,' the old girls shouted from the other side of the door, banging it loudly and kicking it.

'Just as well we're not of your time,' muttered Marta,

in disgust. There was a lot of commotion out there. It seemed as though the whole residence had come to ridicule them. At that time of night, there was no sign of the security staff. The old girls were on the point of breaking down the door and they cowered in fear, until finally, after quite a struggle, Bonitão and Wassi, probably to redeem themselves in Hadjame's eyes, managed to chase the girls away. Hadjame smiled proudly and things returned to normal. Cláudia got back into her own bed and Francisca decided to turn on the light. She pressed the switch repeatedly, but it didn't work. Hadjame was laughing quietly, under her pillow.

'I bet the old girls turned off the power,' Marta concluded, angrily.

'Good night, girls,' said Hadjame, pleased.

4
The Conquest

On the Monday, Hadjame and her schoolfriends were feeling very anxious about the first day of classes. They got up very early for their bath, because they knew that they couldn't take it at the same time as the old girls. They set off for school after breakfast. At school, Hadjame met some of her schoolfriends and teachers. It was a friendlier atmosphere than the disorderly climate of the residence. During break, the four friends met up in the schoolyard, chatting, laughing and making comments about some of the boys that passed until Francisca saw Wassi approaching, Hadjame asked her friends to desist.

'Everything OK, girls?' said Wassi by way of greeting, in a charming voice, as he approached. Francisca sighed, fanning herself, and they all laughed at her. The bell rang and they went their separate ways. The first day of classes wasn't full for Hadjame and Marta, so they both went back to the residence. When they got to their dormitory's door, they stood stock still, thinking they had got the wrong room. While they were away, the old girls had invaded their room and chucked dirty water onto their beds, ripped their sheets, and spread mud all over the place. It was an incredible scene.

'Who did this?' There were tears in Hadjame's eyes at the sight. Those were not any old sheets; they were a gift from her grandmother and they meant a lot to her.

'It has to be the old girls. Let's get some clean sheets from the laundry,' Marta said, trying to console her. The two girls hugged each other.

'But I'm not leaving it at that,' said Hadjame, with disgust. Marta tried to stop her, but she ran out. She bumped into Wassi on the steps. He grabbed her arm to stop her. Hadjame was trembling.

'What's the hurry?' he asked, concerned. 'Sit down and tell me all about it.' They both sat on the steps and she told him, sobbing. Wassi listened to her in silence until she had finished.

'I understand you perfectly,' he said, 'but I advise you not to make a formal complaint. It won't help. They'll only continue tormenting you in the same way, believe me.'

'I don't think that's true. I need to phone my mother. I want to leave this place; I can't stand it any more,' she wailed, in tears.

'Would you like to go for a walk with me, on the beach in the evening?' he suggested to cheer her up. Hadjame was taken by surprise.

'On the beach in the evening?' she asked, holding her breath.

'Yes, it'll help you unwind. Will you come, after supper?' he asked hopefully, looking straight into her eyes.

'OK, I will,' she said shyly, feeling she had no alternative. They gave each other a hug and Wassi went with her to fetch some clean sheets from the laundry. So she didn't make the formal complaint. With Marta's permission, Wassi entered their room. Sitting on Hadjame's bed, he ran his fingers through her hair, and Hadjame fell asleep as he told various stories about the residence. Later, Wassi said goodbye to Marta and left the room quietly, and when Hadjame woke up, it was already supper time. Her friends laughed at her for falling asleep in front of Wassi. Feeling embarrassed, Hadjame didn't want to face Wassi in spite of her promise.

'So, I hear Wassi invited you to go for a walk?' asked Francisca when the four of them were on their way to the canteen.

'He did invite me, yes.' Hadjame didn't seem too keen on the idea anymore.

'Who is this arriving?' Cláudia interrupted in alarm. They all looked at the taxi that had stopped in front of the residence. Two young women got out, and Bonitão gestured to them from some way away, to warn them that these were the old girls of their room arriving.

'I've lost my appetite,' said Cláudia, scared, and she ran back to their room.

'I'm not afraid of them,' said Francisca resolutely.

Let's just be nice to them,' said Hadjame. And the

three of them stood there, smiling at the old girls as they pulled their suitcases from the taxi. 'It's just as well that I'm going out this evening; that way I won't spend much time with them today,' sighed Hadjame, no longer embarrassed to face Wassi. There was a sudden commotion at the residence, with lots of clapping and whistling from all over the place. All the old girls were calling the names 'Marcela' and 'Debora,' in delight. You'd think they were celebrities arriving.

'Hey, new girls—go and help the old girls!' they shouted. The three approached timidly and greeted them.

'Is this how you greet the old girls? Go on, give us two kisses,' ordered the one who might have been Marcela. 'Start by telling us your names. And ages,' she said, having fun, while they all looked on, including Wassi, who headed for the canteen. He didn't want to stop and witness this humiliating scene.

'Fifteen! All babies,' exclaimed Marcela when she heard their ages. 'Go on now, pick up our suitcases and take them up.' Debora just laughed. The new girls took the heavy suitcases up to the dormitory. Cláudia had totally disappeared under her sheets and was pretending to be asleep.

'And who's this one, asleep?' asked Marcela, shaking her. Cláudia's plan had failed. She introduced herself shyly; at fourteen, she was the youngest of the four.

'I'll bet you're virgins, too; aren't you?' asked Marcela, in an insinuating voice. The four girls didn't know what to say. 'Are you dumb?' she insisted, frightening them.

'Yes, we are,' replied Marta, feeling humiliated. Cláudia began to cry. The two old girls laughed uproariously.

'Yes you're dumb, or yes you're virgins? What are you crying for?' Marcela was enjoying herself. 'What were your parents thinking, sending you here? Are they tired of you?'

'Leave the little girls alone,' Debora intervened at last. She had lost interest and was putting away her things. They had an entire kifato each to themselves for their clothes, and there were only two available. Hadjame couldn't wait for the time for her walk with Wassi to come. Later, they all went off to have supper, except for Hadjame who didn't want to suffer any more humiliation that day and wanted to make the most of a peaceful moment to tidy herself up. Before the old girls returned from the canteen, she had already left the room, and while talking with some other new girls from the other rooms, she was waiting anxiously in the corridor for Wassi. When they all came back from the canteen, they found her there. Debora wanted to know where she was going and with whom, all tarted up like that.

'I'm going out with Wassi,' replied Hadjame timidly. Marcela couldn't contain herself from laughing.

'Pay no attention to Marcela. Wassi is a good lad,' said Debora, defending him.

'Don't go falling for him; he's a womaniser,' shouted Marcela when she saw Wassi approaching.

'Why does she say that?' asked Hadjame, puzzled, as Wassi greeted her with a kiss on each cheek.

'Take no notice of her. Marcela's always a bit of a joker. I brought you some dessert; I didn't see you at supper tonight,' he said. He gave her an apple and Hadjame thanked him with a smile. 'Shall we go?' he suggested, and she agreed. They left the residence and walked until the beach. Hand in hand, they walked towards the waterside road. They decided to stop and buy ice cream at the esplanade. Hadjame asked for a chocolate ice cream and Wassi followed her choice. Sitting on a pavement bench, they savoured their ice cream as the lights of the town reflected like diamonds on the sand. To the sound of the waves, with a light breeze blowing into their faces, on that moonlit night, the two of them chatted relaxedly for hours. They spoke of their families, their plans, their likes and dislikes. 'For the first time, here was someone who didn't ridicule my real age,' thought Hadjame.

'And you must be at least eighteen, like Xissola,' she guessed.

'That's right. I'm actually eighteen years old,' he said with a friendly smile. 'Do you want to walk on the sand for a bit?' he suggested. Hadjame tried to refuse, but he pulled her with him until they were right by the sea. They were suddenly soaked by a big wave, from the waist down.

'You'll pay for this, Wassi,' she said, wet through. Running after him as he fled, Hadjame finally gave up in exhaustion. She sat on the sand. Wassi came and joined her, both trying to get their breath back, laughing, feeling at ease with one another.

'Can I smell your perfume?' he asked suddenly. 'Only if you want me to, of course,' he said, with a mischievous smile. Hadjame quickly leant against him and Wassi breathed in her perfume. 'Sweet and gentle, like its owner,' he said.

'Thank you. Xissola gave it to me,' she said shyly. And they looked at each other in silence. Wassi drew close to her to kiss her and she moved away.

'Shall we go?' she finally suggested embarrassed. Wassi threw her a smile, and saying nothing, he courteously helped her up. They shook the sand off their clothes and walked back to the residence, which was very quiet because it was a weekday. It was almost midnight, so Hadjame didn't want to spend anymore time chatting with him. She hastily thanked him for the invitation and hugged him goodbye.

'Goodnight, princess,' Wassi said. With a warm gaze, he watched her go.

In Hadjame's room, all the girls were already asleep. The lights were out. 'By order of the old girls', she thought happily. She tiptoed in silently and got ready for bed. Marta felt the vibration from her bunk when Hadjame climbed up into the top one.

'How did it go?' she asked in almost a whisper.

'I'll tell you tomorrow,' whispered Hadjame. 'Goodnight,' she said as she lay in her bed, thinking about Wassi, until she fell asleep. In the following couple of months it was the same routine. Wassi tried incessantly to gain Hadjame's heart, while she turned her focus to her education. To the four girls' amusement, Debora and Marcela sympathized with them. Both even protected the girls against all sorts of anarchy they could face. They did not allow anyone to touch their "little babies', as they used to refer to them.

5
The First Kiss

After the entire nine months of the academic year, in which they had faced all kinds of challenges, things finally seemed to return to normal. When they were all getting ready for the long-awaited end-of-term dance, it was as though it were only yesterday that they had been the scared new girls. They recalled their worst experiences with the old students over the nine months, but now it was all in the past, it was all over. Now they were all one big family, without distinction, but when it came to a party, Hadjame was always the last to be ready.

'What are you going to do now that Wassi is leaving?' asked Francisca, while Hadjame was rummaging through her disordered suitcase for the best thing to wear to the party.

'And you haven't even given him a kiss. You awkward girl,' said Marta, insinuatingly.

'You never know; it might happen tonight!' said Hadjame slyly as she picked up a red dress from her suitcase and tried it on.

'And what about you, Marta, are you going to the party with Bonitão?' asked Debora, curious.

'Just as friends of course, whereas Hadjame and Wassi…' Marta said defensively.

'Very good friends, I suppose you mean,' said Hadjame to provoke her.

'Hadjame stop talking and get yourself ready, Wassi is going to be here in a minute to pick you up,' Cláudia warned her.

'She's always last,' Marta smiled. Everyone else was already at the exit.

'Wait for me; I can't find anything decent to wear. Oh, God!' wailed Hadjame. Kindly, Cláudia suggested the red dress that she had already discarded, and they all agreed.

'Wassi's here. He looks so smart,' said Marcela emphatically from the door.

'Tell him I'm just coming—five minutes,' replied Hadjame, disconcerted. She finally put on the red dress voted for by the majority and went out to meet her partner for the evening.

'Awww! You look lovely, princess,' exclaimed Wassi when he stared at her in the short red dress, which left her shapely legs visible, for the first time, a little above the knee. Open at the back, and with a low neck at the front of the bodice, it clung to her body, giving her a perfect silhouette. 'You'll be the prettiest girl at the party,' he said, impressed.

'Don't be modest; you look pretty smart yourself,' said Hadjame in return for the praise. Wassi was wearing a white polo shirt under his brown jacket, faded blue jeans on those athletic legs, and his sneakers. The whole look, especially the colour of his jacket, made him look like a seducer out of a novel, and he wore irresistible aftershave. With a mischievous smile, Wassi held out his arm in an arc, and Hadjame linked arms with him. The good music they could hear clearly as they approached the hall heralded a promising night. Without further delay, they got out of the taxi and went into party. They greeted their friends and Hadjame went straight onto the dance floor with her girlfriends, where they danced tirelessly. Wassi watched her sensuous movements discreetly.

'Wassi can't take his eyes off you,' Marta shouted in her ear. Hadjame waved to him, and continued dancing provocatively. He barely smiled. They danced without stopping all evening, until Hadjame decided to get some air. She left her friends and went out of the hall, and Wassi followed her.

'Tired now?' he whispered in her ear, startling her. 'Sorry, I didn't mean to make you jump, but all alone in the street at this time of night, little one?' he teased.

'I know how to look after myself,' she said, wiping her face with a paper napkin.

'I was beginning to think you weren't going to stop all night.'

'I love dancing; it makes me feel good. If you like, I'll

show you,' she offered, strutting up and down in front of him.

'Only if it's now,' said Wassi provocatively. Excited, he grasped her gently round the waist, and pulled her to him. Hadjame felt her heart beating fast and, to the sound of Roberto Carlos, she let Wassi lift her up while they danced. He breathed fast into the nape of her neck, and this made her shudder. She asked him to stop, but he had already gone too far to stop. Gently Wassi caressed her perfect tanned face, and drew the outline of her mouth with the tips of his fingers. Hadjame followed it all with her eyes closed. Cautiously, he drew close to her mouth and touched her gently with his lips. Suddenly, Hadjame had no air and thought she would faint. She turned her head around, and like two thirsty people quenching their thirst, they kissed intensely for the first time, on that moonlit night, and swore eternal love for each other. They went back inside the hall, and danced together all night long, until the party finished, and they both announced to their friends that they were in a relationship. Their friends congratulated them. They all went back to the residence, where most of the people were packing their suitcases ready to leave in the next few hours, without even sleeping for a little while. Everybody seemed so excited while they shouted and ran the entire corridor. The most excited ones were those who'd completed their studies. They did the most bizarre things anyone could imagine, including running completely naked from one dormitory to another, and the girls couldn't stop screaming. The entire residence went crazy. Everybody started singing at once in a very loud voice and shaking their dormitories doors, which almost fell down. Wassi and Hadjame were talking in the corridor, watching and laughing at everyone's behaviour. It was always good to go back home after so long. Everyone was about to travel to their own hometowns, and most of them would see each other again only after the end of their holidays.

6

The Holidays

On the first Friday of Hadjame's holidays, she and Chimene were taken by Kizua to the house of their grandmother. Wassi, Marta, and Xissola were Hadjame's guests for lunch with her grandmother. Hadjame thought it would be easier to take them to her grandma's house because Grandma always liked to have her house full of people, and later on, she could help Hadjame talk about Wassi to her mother, who still didn't know of his existence. To Hadjame's delight, Kizua wouldn't be staying with them, as he had arranged to meet some friends.

'I'll pick you up later,' he said as he left. The two sisters went into the house, where they found Grandma in the kitchen with the maid, preparing some delicacies. They greeted her and lent a hand preparing the food.

'You're going to love meeting Wassi,' said Hadjame to her sister and grandma, while she made an orange cake. Later on, the three guests arrived, driven by Wassi, who was made very welcome by Hadjame's family.

'Nice meeting you Wassi,' said Chimene, looking him up and down as if he was being classified.

'Let's eat before the food gets cold,' Grandma suggested.

'My Grandma makes the best feijoada[6] in the world,' boasted Hadjame. They all went to sit down at the table.

'Now, Wassi, tell us more about yourself,' Grandma said as they ate.

'Well,' he began, clearing his throat, 'I'm an only child; my parents are separated. I live with my dad, and my mother lives in England…'

'Hadjame's father is in England too, working,' said Grandma.

'If all goes well, we'll be going there to see him,' said Chimene.

'I hate England's weather,' complained Marta.

'Me too,' Hadjame agreed. Xissola seemed very subdued, so Chimene spoke to her.

'What's up, Xissola? Don't you have anything to say?'

'Me?… I agree with you,' she said, having totally lost the thread of the conversation. They all laughed at her, making her uncomfortable. The orange cake was served as dessert, and Hadjame bragged about making it.

'Grandma helped, too,' Chimene pointed out.

'It looks delicious,' commented Wassi, hoping to ward

6 A stew of beans with beef and pork.

off a fight between the sisters. Hadjame cut a slice and gave it to him. 'Ummmm, it's lovely. I'm going to ask for the recipe for my Dad.' They all laughed. The conversation went on, and Marta took the opportunity to invite her friends to the opening of her father's new restaurant at the beautiful Island of Luanda in the next day. They all agreed to go, except for Chimene, who was too young.

'I'm fourteen now,' Chimene complained, and they all laughed at her. After lunch, they spent the afternoon watching a comedy film, and later on, Kizua came to pick them up in the car. He got out to greet Grandma, and Hadjame introduced him to Wassi.

'Pleased to meet you,' Kizua said in a cold voice.

'Come back again soon,' said Grandma to them all.

'We certainly will, Grandma. Your meal was lovely,' said Wassi, kissing her on both cheeks.

'I told you that you'd enjoy meeting my Grandma,' said Hadjame, pleased with the outcome of the lunch.

'Tomorrow at 2 PM at the restaurant,' Marta reminded them, as she said goodbye to her friend. Wassi took the two girls home. Hadjame was very disappointed with her brother. Kizua said she was too young to have a boyfriend, and she didn't agree. They couldn't agree on anything and were still arguing when they got home.

'What's going on?' asked their mother.

'Ask your daughter. Someone needs to take some

control in this house while father is away,' muttered Kizua, going off to his room angrily. Hadjame wept with disappointment and confessed her mother all about it.

'A brother's jealousy,' was all her mother said. To her amazement, there was no lecture. Hadjame wanted to kiss Kizua, as he'd ended up helping her to broach the subject of Wassi with her mother in a most easy way.

7
The Jealousy

Hadjame spotted several old friends at the new restaurant, and whenever they came over to the table to greet her she kept getting up. Wassi looked on in silence, feeling jealous, until Xissola asked him to dive into the deep blue sea.

'Looks like Wassi isn't enjoying your popularity,' Marta whispered into her ear. Hadjame shrugged her shoulders as if to say, 'What can I do?' She didn't want to upset Wassi, but she wasn't going to ignore her friends either.

'Don't you think Hadjame's a bit free with her attentions?' Xissola asked Wassi, as they swam.

'Not really,' he replied, trying to cover up his jealousy.

'I gather she has lots of friends at the residence, too.'

'What are you implying?' he asked, irritated.

'Just a thought,' she said.

I've had enough. Let's go home,' he said annoyed.

Xissola didn't know what to say. They swam back to shore.

'Calm down, Wassi. Sorry, I didn't mean anything, I swear,' said Xissola running towards him trying to apologise.

'Going home already?' Hadjame asked, puzzled, when they returned to the table.

'Yes, It's almost 6 PM I'm feeling tired, and I've got a lot on tomorrow,' he said, apologetically.

'That's OK,' Hadjame said, although she wasn't convinced. They said goodbye to Marta, and all three of them left. They travelled in silence, just listening to the music in the car, until Hadjame was the first to be dropped off.

'Goodnight,' Hadjame said to Wassi and Xissola.

'Goodnight,' Wassi replied coldly. As she went up the stairs, Hadjame bumped into Chimene who was with a boy almost her age. Chimene was startled to see her sister and waved the boy away. She ran after Hadjame, pretending to be relaxed, asking about the party. Without asking her anything about the boy, Hadjame told her all about it, including Wassi's attitude.

'He must have been jealous,' Chimene concluded. They both smiled.

'Who was that boy?' asked Hadjame finally, unable to contain herself.

‘A friend,’ replied Chimene shortly. ‘You shouldn’t have let Wassi take Xissola home alone,’ her sister said, changing the subject.

‘As you might know, Xissola is my best friend.’

‘But she’s got more experience than you.’

‘Please, Chimene, don’t start.’

‘What are you two coming in arguing about?’interrupted their mother when they got into the house.

‘Your daughter here was with a boy on the stairs,’ Hadjame complained.

‘You were with Wassi who left with Xissola. I’m fourteen now, and I’m not as naive as you are,’ Chimene said to provoke her.

‘Listen, little brat, I’m sixteen, and you’ll always be the youngest,’ said Hadjame, irritated. She was on the point of slapping her sister, but was prevented by her mother.

‘So you’ve sunk to arguing over boys in the house?’ their mother scolded them.

‘I’m going to my room,’ said Hadjame, really annoyed.

‘Me, too,’ said Chimene.

‘Before you go little girl, I want you to tell me what’s going on, right now,’ their mother said, waiting for an explanation from Chimene.

'He's just a friend, Mum, I swear,' said Chimene, noticing her mother's seriousness. 'You know that I want to meet an English boy, tall and fair with blue eyes,' she added in her defence. Her mother burst out laughing at her daughter's fantasy, and she allowed her to go to her room finally. On the other side of the room lying on her bed, on the phone to Wassi, Hadjame apologised, saying that she couldn't ignore her friends. He understood, and it all went back to normal. He invited her to eat with him in the same restaurant, just the two of them, followed by the cinema, the next day, to make up for what had happened, and they said goodbye affectionately, like young lovers.

The next morning, during Sunday breakfast, their mother asked Hadjame to tell her more about Wassi, and Hadjame told her all about him. Chimene seemed resentful and was not talking to her older sister.

'I'm going out for dinner with him today, and afterwards we're going to the cinema,' Hadjame said excitedly.

'This family only seems to have one topic of conversation. Soon Chimene's going to start too,' complained Kizua, banging his cutlery on the table. He went out.

'Why me?' Chimene asked puzzled. Their mother shook her head at her son's attitude. Hadjame cut an apple in half and gave it to her sister as a peace offering.

'I need your father here. It's just as well that he's asked us all to go there soon, because you lot are driving me mad,' said their mother.

'I can't wait to meet those lovely English guys,' said Chimene, simply. And she bit into the apple, relaxed. Hadjame, her mother and Maria looked at each other in amazement, but didn't say a word.

8

The First Row

Hadjame waited anxiously for Wassi for their Sunday night date. Then, carrying a box of chocolates, Wassi arrived to pick up his girlfriend, looking very smart as always. Hadjame, too, was dressed up in a light print dress and flat sandals. With all the neighbours looking on, she went out to his car and they left for the Jango restaurant. Wassi parked his car, asked some car washers, young lads who normally hung around the door of the restaurant checking the cars, to keep an eye on it, and the two of them went into the restaurant arm in arm.

'I brought you here so we could have a serious talk,' he explained. He pulled out a chair for her to sit down, and Hadjame thanked him. 'You'll be going back to the residence soon, and things will be different between us.'

'Different, how?' Hadjame asked.

'Well, I know you have lots of friends,' he said calmly.

'And what of it?'

‘Calm down,’ Wassi said, gesturing to the waiter.

‘You don’t trust me?’ she asked impatiently.

‘It’s not that. What I really want to say to you is that since you’re going away, and I’m staying…’ he went on, while Hadjame listened to him in silence.

‘Then I’m going to go off with one of my friends, is that it?’ she broke in, furious.

‘Calm down, Hadjame, please. It’s not that at all,’ said Wassi, angry with himself for not finding the right words.

‘Then what is it? All this time with you, I thought you had more trust in me.’

‘Hadjame, please, I only…’

‘Take me home, please,’ she asked angrily.

‘But Hadjame, our evening has hardly started. I swear that…’

‘Take me home, please. You’ve ruined my evening.’ Hadjame stood up suddenly and headed for the car. Wassi cancelled the order and followed her out. He tipped the boy who was watching the car and they left. Hadjame was more intent on looking out of the car window than hearing anything he had to say. Wassi tried to apologise all the way back, but she blocked her ears until they got to her building. She opened the car door brusquely and ran to her apartment, ignoring his calls.

'What's happened?' her mother asked in concern as Hadjame rushed past her and shut herself in her room. Disappointed, Wassi tried to ring her as he arrived home, but she didn't want to answer.

'Well, aren't you going to answer your phone?' asked her mother, who had come into her room to talk.

'No, Mum, I don't want to talk to him.'

'You should at least listen to what he has to say,' said Chimene, who'd joined them in Hadjame's room.

'I'd have thought you'd be on my side. Goodnight,' she said, annoyed, and her mother and sister left her room. She cried all night, and despite all of Wassi's attempts to apologise, she definitely didn't want to see him again or answer his calls until the day she went back to school. He phoned and Chimene informed him that Hadjame had just left. Wassi couldn't believe what he was hearing. A week before she left, he was still hoping that things would get back to normal, and now she had left without even saying goodbye. He felt deeply hurt.

'I'm really sorry, Wassi. My sister is a bit of a hard nut,' Chimene said, trying to console him. But he found no consolation in her words. He felt dejected. 'And who's there with you?' asked Chimene, curious. 'I can hear voices.'

'Xissola,' he replied without emotion. Xissola had gone round to help him after he had phoned her in the hope she could convince her friend, but now it was too late. Hadjame had already left.

'Xissola doesn't waste any time,' Chimene muttered under her breath.

'What?' asked Wassi, who hadn't heard. At that moment, his mind was on Hadjame's childishness.

'Give her a kiss from me,' said Chimene, to cover up. And they said goodbye. Wassi was sad and disappointed at Hadjame's behaviour.

'Don't be like that, Wassi. Give her a bit longer,' Xissola said, trying to console her upset friend. 'How about going to the cinema with me this evening, there is a new movie which is out today' she suggested promptly.

'I think that's just what I need,' he agreed. They gave each other a hug, and he thanked her for her support. That evening they went to the cinema, and by coincidence they ran into Chimene and Kizua who were coming from the seven o'clock sitting. They went over to greet Hadjame's brother and sister.

'So Chimene, have you heard from your sister yet?' asked Wassi hopefully, ignoring the rudeness of Kizua, who didn't even shake hands in greeting.

'She's been in touch, yes. But I think she's still miserable.'

'It can't be easy for her,' said Xissola.

'Yes, and it's a bit dangerous for her, don't you think?' concluded Chimene. The atmosphere grew tense, on top of Kizua's coldness, so Wassi moved off to buy their tickets.

'What's wrong with you, girl? You need to grow up and then you can talk to me, OK?' said Xissola, angrily. She barely said goodbye to Kizua who was talking to some other friends, and went off to see Wassi. They went into the nine o'clock sitting. At the first opportunity, Chimene rang her sister and told her all about it. Hadjame was upset that Xissola hadn't told her anything about going out with Wassi, as they both always kept in touch. Feeling jealous and betrayed, Hadjame stopped answering her friend's calls, too. After that, Wassi and Xissola went out together quite often. Time passed and the distance between all three grew. Xissola became her ex-best friend, and after so many attempts to apologise, without any success, Wassi went off to study in England at his mother's invitation. Strangely, when he started living closer to Kizua's Unite Student Accomodation in London, the two young men finally became good friends.

9
The Decision

All went very well. Finally, at age eighteen, Hadjame had just passed the final project for her high school diploma in social sciences. Her family was there to congratulate her, mother, sister, and grandmother. Xissola was there too, taking the opportunity of this happy event to make things up with Hadjame. Acknowledging her childishness at the time, Hadjame forgave her friend and things went back to normal. There were times when she wished Wassi were there, but she resigned herself to the support of her family and friends. With her bags already packed, they were all planning to go back to Luanda that night with the driver. The dangers of the civil war were no longer imminent, and many people found it more peaceful to travel at night. The journey brought to her mind the first time Hadjame had travelled on those roads, pictures she would never be able to get out of her head. Anxious, and with only a few months to go before their trip to England, her mother and sister talked of nothing else all the way home.

'Why won't you change your mind and come with us?' her mother asked.

'I'd rather stay with Grandma. I'll take the opportunity to go with her to South Africa for her surgery,' she said, hugging her grandmother with affection.

'And what about university? There are still three months before our trip; you'll still have plenty of time to decide after you come back from South Africa.'

Please, Mum, don't make me,' she begged.

'Your father won't like this at all,' her mother reminded her.

'But I've already decided,' Hadjame complained, as though, turning eighteen, she was capable of knowing what was best for her. Through the window, she said goodbye to the place where she had spent three years of her life. Marta was going to the United States to join her family, which was always on the move. Bonitão, Marta's boyfriend, was already there on a two-year grant, making everything easy for them. Cláudia and Francisca were going back to their home provinces and it would be very difficult to keep in touch with them. They had not heard any more of Marcela and Debora; the latest news was that Debora had married a Frenchman, and was living in Paris, and Marcela was working in an oil company in Cabinda's Province. Hadjame would miss the good times and the friends she had made at school, but life moved on.

'When's Grandma's trip precisely?' asked Xissola curiously.

'Next week. I'm going for three weeks,' Grandma replied.

'Did you know that Wassi will also be back next week, on holiday for three months, Hadjame?' said Xissola, who always kept in touch with her friend, even when he was far away. Hadjame could not manage to control her heart, which began to beat faster when she heard his name.

'Wassi's in England. That's why she doesn't want to go there mum,' said Chimene, reading her thoughts.

'You still haven't got over that young man? I thought that was a passing fancy,' said her mother. 'You'll find someone better; you're still very young.'

'Would you get back with him?' asked Chimene provocatively. At sixteen, she thought she had the world at her feet and was concerned only about parties, shopping, and going out with friends almost everyday. This was driving the entire family mad. She was the black sheep of the family.

'Leave your sister in peace, Chimene!' her mother chided her. In silence, Hadjame was imagining how it would be to meet Wassi again after two long years. She felt as though deep down she was still waiting for him to come back. She often blamed herself for her past childishness, and now it was already too late. 'He probably already found someone else,' she thought. It was 2 AM when they finally arrived in Luanda. She always felt good when she was back home. Hadjame went to find Maria, who had made an early morning supper to greet them. Hadjame rushed into the maid's arms to catch up with her, and ate as if she were starving. It was a while since she had eaten so well.

They chatted for a while, and then they all went to bed. Xissola slept in their house, to bring Hadjame up to date with all the gossip. Xissola told her that she had lots of boyfriends but she didn't want relationships; she preferred to be free. In spite of the danger it involved, Hadjame sometimes wished she was as uninhibited as her friend, but she was very sentimental and became too attached to things, which is why she never forgot her first love, Wassi. With no time to lose, Hadjame already had started to look for the best universities for psychology in town, and the day of the trip to South Africa with her Grandma had finally arrived. Her mother was stuck in a traffic jam, unable to get there on time, so Xissola, who had recently passed her driving test, would probably take them to the airport.

'But why don't you go with the driver? It would be safer,' said her mother on the phone, worried.

'Don't worry Auntie. I'll be really careful behind the wheel,' shouted Xissola, aware of Dona Mónica's concern. The three girls set off to fetch Grandma. They apologised for their mother's absence and set off for the airport where, after checking in, they sat chatting at a restaurant table. Hadjame was very anxious about Wassi, who was due to arrive that day, but she would rather keep it to herself than share her thoughts with Xissola or Chimene.

'Hey, everybody, look over there. It's the flight from England coming in,' Xissola broke in, pointing at the arrivals board.

'I think you still might manage to see him,' said Chimene, reading her thoughts.

'Let's change the subject, please,' said Hadjame, feigning a lack of interest, but her hands were sweating at the possibility of seeing Wassi again.

'OK, let's talk about your trip to England with us,' suggested Chimene pointedly. Grandma was sitting quietly, watching her granddaughters arguing.

'I've already said I'm not going to England. I'd rather stay with my beloved grandma.' Getting up from her chair, Hadjame went and gave her grandma a hug. Their flight was leaving soon, she thought sadly as she heard her flight called. Saying goodbye to her sister and friend, Hadjame and her grandma went and joined the queue at emigration. Hadjame looked anxiously around her.

'Is everything all right, my dear?' asked her grandmother.

'I'm fine, Grandma,' she said, covering up. And when she least expected it, she heard someone calling her name. Recognising his voice, Hadjame broke through the crowd and ran to meet Wassi, leaving her grandma standing there with her ticket in her hand.

'Aren't you going to give me a hug, princess?' Wassi asked, with the roguish smile she knew, which he hadn't lost with the passing of time. He looked more attractive than ever.

'Wassi? I thought that…' She tried to speak.

'Shhhhh,' Wassi interrupted her, and he gave her a big hug.

'I've missed you so much,' she whispered in his ear, trembling.

'I've missed you terribly, too, my love. You look even lovelier,' he said, admiringly. There were tears in both their eyes, and they clung to each other.

'I'm really sorry,' said Hadjame. Touching her lips, Wassi kissed her gently. Then they said goodbye and he wished her bon voyage, saying that he would wait anxiously for her return.

10

The Betrayal

One week after Hadjame left, carrying a bottle of red wine in his hand for dinner, Wassi found himself at Xissola's door ringing the bell. Xissola has told him she had something very important to tell him. She came to meet her friend, kissed him on both cheeks and invited him in.

'And your mother?' asked Wassi, curious, looking all around the lounge.

'Oh I forgot to tell you. My mother's away, Wassi thought it a bit strange, but said nothing.

'So, what's up?' asked Wassi.

'Relax. Let's eat first,' said Xissola, she took the wine from him and went off to heat the food in the microwave. She went back into the lounge. 'What would you like to listen to?' she asked, selecting several CDs.

'Roberto Carlos,' he suggested. Xissola put on the Roberto Carlos CD, and let things take their course. She served the meal, bringing dishes of cod with cream in from the kitchen.

'Now are you going to let me know what this important thing is you had to tell me?'

'No hurry. I'll tell you after we've eaten. 'Do you like the food? This dish is my speciality,' she boasted, changing the subject.

'The food's lovely. Thanks,' he said.

'Would you like a little more wine?' she asked. Proposing a toast, Xissola added more wine to her friend's glass, and ate silently. When it was time for dessert, they sat on the sofa in the lounge and ate a fruit salad, watching a film on the TV.

'Come on, then, tell me all about it,' he asked insistently.

'I don't want to look bad in front of Hadjame,' she began, creating a sense of suspense.

'How so?' Wassi moved closer to her, so he could hear her better.

'I think it's unfair that she didn't tell you the truth at the airport one week ago.'

'It was all so fast,' said Wassi. 'But We have been keeping in touch everyday.' At that moment his phone rang. 'Sorry, it's Hadjame; I'm going to answer.'

'Do as you please,' said Xissola with disdain in her face. Wassi spoke with Hadjame, and they were both very happy. Hadjame wanted to know where he was. Xissola made a sign to her friend not to tell her the truth. A bit confused, the words came out of his mouth.

'At Xissola's,' he said, against his friend's will.

'That's nice. Give her and Auntie Sofia my love,' said Hadjame.

'Aunt Sofia is away, but do you want to talk to Xissola?' he said innocently. It all felt very strange to Hadjame, but she did not mention anything and agreed to talk to Xissola, and Wassi handed her the phone.

'Oh, Xi! How are things? Are you taking good care of Wassi for me?' she joked innocently.

'Of course I am. Relax, he's in good hands,' said Xissola.

'I know. I have so much news to tell you about me and Wassi,' said Hadjame enthusiastically, 'but I'll tell you all about it in two weeks when I get home.'

'I can't wait! I'm going to pass you to Wassi now.' Xissola handed him the phone and he said goodbye cheerfully to his girlfriend. After the phone call, they looked at each other in silence, not knowing what to say.

'Why didn't you want her to know I was here? What's going on?' Wassi finally asked.

'I'm going to get us some more wine,' said Xissola, changing the subject and acting mysterious.

'Don't you think we've drunk too much already?'. Taking no notice of her friend's words, with a sly smile, Xissola went to fetch more wine from the table and while he wasn't looking, slipped a sleeping pill into his glass.

'Forgive me, my friend,' she murmured in a quiet voice, thinking of Hadjame. In spite of her conscience, she gave the glass to Wassi, who drank from it unaware. There were tears in her eyes as she watched him drinking.

'Now sit down and tell me all about it.' Wassi pulled her, and, off-balance and leaning on her, said, yawning, 'I think I've had too much to drink. I feel really sleepy all of a sudden. I'd better go home, but tomorrow,' he yawned again, 'tomorrow, you're going to tell me all about it,' he said, stumbling over his words. 'I love your friend very…' Wassi fell asleep like a log on the living-room sofa. Slowly unbuttoning his shirt, Xissola began stroking his chest, and after a while she dragged him to her room, where they slept together.

The next morning, Xissola brought him breakfast while he was sleeping. Carelessly, she tripped with the tray, and dropped the cutlery on the floor.

'Sorry, I woke you up, but I've made you strong coffee. It'll do you good,' she said, relaxedly. Bewildered to see Xissola in front of him, Wassi leapt straight out of bed.

'Where am I?' he asked, lost. He looked around him, and realised he was not in his room. 'My head,' he complained.

'Calm down, Wassi. Good morning,' she said, leaning over to give him a kiss. Wassi pushed her away brusquely, grabbed his clothes from the floor, and rummaged around for his car keys.

'Will you just explain to me what's going on?' he asked, gripping her tightly by the arms. He shook her angrily.

'Stop it, please! You're hurting me. Last night was wonderful. We did everything, my love,' said Xissola emphatically. Wassi was about to slap her, but instead flung her onto the bed, and went on searching for his car keys.

'Hadjame, Hadjame, always Hadjame,' Xissola burst out. 'She left you for two years and didn't want to have anything to do with you. I've always been there to console you,' she wailed, weeping bitterly.

'You've gone quite mad, Xissola,' said Wassi as he found his keys. 'I'd better go now, before I lose my head.'

Xissola ran after him, crying that she loved him, but Wassi left. She tried ringing him several times that day, but he didn't answer.

11

The Invitation

'Tomorrow? Is something up?' Wassi asked Chimene on the phone.

'Cool it, Wassi. My mother just wants to say hello and get to know you personally,' said Chimene. Wassi felt a chill in his stomach when he thought about meeting Hadjame's mother for the first time, and while Hadjame was not there. When he thought back over the previous night with Xissola, he was very ill at ease; he felt like an adolescent.

'OK, I'll come tomorrow then,' he agreed at last.

'We'll expect you for lunch with us tomorrow. Is that a deal?'

'It's a deal.'

'By the way, how did dinner with Xissola go? Hadjame told me.'

'Fine,' replied Wassi shortly.

'Ummmm, I see. See you tomorrow then,' Chimene said

not convinced. They said goodbye. Wassi's heart was beating hard. He didn't answer Xissola, who called him more than a hundred times, and he didn't sleep at all that night, wondering what could be so important that Dona Mónica should invite him around in Hadjame's absence. He considered backing out, but he didn't want to offend his girlfriend's family.

The next day, he arrived at the time arranged, carrying a chocolate cake for dessert, one of the ones he knew Chimene loved.

'Well, Wassi, how are you?' Dona Mónica greeted him. Wassi felt the heat rise up through his body. It was the first time he had met with Hadjame's mother and it all felt very strange.

'I'm fine, thank you, Dona Mónica,' he replied shyly, and then he greeted Chimene, who thanked him for the cake. She took it into the kitchen and told Maria that she could serve lunch at any time.

'On Saturdays, we always have mufete[7] at home. I hope you like it,' said Dona Mónica, ushering him in with a friendly smile.

'Of course I do. My friend Bonitão always says Saturday isn't Saturday without mufete,' joked Wassi, relaxing.

'I know Bonitão. He's studying in the United States, isn't he?' asked Dona Mónica and he nodded. 'Now then, Wassi! The fact is, I invited you here to get to know you better and to talk about your relationship

7 A typical Angolan fish dish with cassava, sweet potato and plantain.

with my daughter.' Wassi held his breath. A thousand and one things went through his mind.

'Is there a problem, Dona Mónica?' he asked, alarmed.

'Don't worry! Everything is fine. But she spoke to me on the phone, and I get the impression that she's very keen to revive this romance when she gets back. So I want to know what your real intentions are, after all the things that have gone on between you.' Wassi sighed with relief.

'I appreciate your concern, Dona Mónica. As you know, I've always liked your daughter very much...'

'Only now you are living in England, from what I hear,' Dona Mónica interrupted him, serious.

'Convince her to come with us. Then you'll have your girlfriend near you,' said Chimene, helping Maria lay the table. Her mother looked her up and down with a serious expression on her face.

'I perfectly understand. But I like Hadjame very much, and I would never hurt her,' he went on, timidly.

'So I should hope. Hadjame is a very sensitive girl,' said her mother.

'Sensitive, and a daydreamer too,' added Chimene. Maria nudged her with her elbow.

'Be quiet, Chimene,' her mother chided her.

'Lunch is served,' Maria announced, to Chimene's relief.

'I'll give you my vote of confidence, although her father and brother don't agree. But I'm her mother,' she said, as she invited him to sit at the table.

'I'm very grateful for that, Dona Mónica,' he said, feeling that time was standing still. Sitting at the table, Wassi told them about his experiences abroad and the difficulties he was having in adapting to some things, such as the climate and the food. But he also said that he was getting used to it and that he found England a great place to live, encouraging the family further. It was all going really well until Chimene decided to bring up the subject of the dinner with Xissola again, causing Wassi to choke badly on his food. Terrified, Dona Mónica called Maria to bring a glass of water, quickly. Wassi felt relieved after drinking the water, when all of a sudden Chimene broke into an uncontrollable laugh that she could not control. Embarrassed, Wassi apologised for the upset he'd caused and things went back to normal. After lunch, and feeling more relaxed with the family, Wassi got a phone call from home, telling him that his father had been rushed to hospital after suffering a heart attack. He said goodbye hastily to Hadjame's family, happy in part because the meeting between Hadjame's mother and him was over, and otherwise sad because of his father's news. He drove to the hospital. With no time to lose, Chimene rang her sister to tell her all about it and a little more besides.

'And he even choked on his food when I mentioned him having dinner with Xissola,' she said pointedly.

'Chimene, please,' said her sister. Chimene's versions of events were always exaggerated.

'Don't say I didn't warn you,' muttered Chimene. Hadjame rang Wassi after her sister's conversation. Happily, his father was out of danger, in spite of the fright he had given everyone.

'Why don't you ring Xi. It'll be good for you to have someone there to give you support,' Hadjame suggested. Wassi disagreed automatically. The last thing he wanted just then was to see Xissola again.

12

The Confession

Hadjame and her grandmother arrived on a Saturday at 6.30 PM. The whole family, including Wassi and Xissola, were going to meet them at the airport. Wassi was making his own way to the airport, while Xissola was going with Hadjame's family. Although the presence of Xissola at that time was still uncomfortable for him, he was so keen to see his girlfriend again that nothing, absolutely nothing, not even Xissola, was going to spoil that moment. On the way to the airport, the three of them decided to stop at a florist's. Wassi spotted Dona Mónica's car parked and stopped there too, and he went to meet them. He decided to buy some flowers for his girlfriend too.

'Good afternoon,' he greeted Hadjame's mother and sister politely, ignoring Xissola's presence. Wassi chatted with Dona Mónica and helped her choose the best flower arrangements they had. Xissola felt very sad about the situation, and they continued on to the airport in their separate cars. At the airport, Wassi kept himself apart the whole time, avoiding any contact with Xissola. They were like two untouchables.

'Wassi really likes Hadjame, don't you think, Xi?' asked Chimene, while they were waiting anxiously for her sister and Grandma to arrive.

'He does,' Xissola agreed briefly, with tears in her eyes.

'Why are you crying, my dear?' asked Dona Mónica, full of concern.

'I'll be back in a minute, Auntie. I feel a bit sick,' Xissola said, ignoring her question. In front of the mirror in the toilets, she burst into tears.

'I think she must be excited about seeing her friend again,' Dona Mónica said to Chimene, smiling. Chimene nodded. Dona Mónica called Wassi over to join them. He approached timidly, relieved that Xissola had gone off. It was a very tense and anxious moment for him.

'Telling her the whole truth yourself would be the best thing to do, my son,' his father's advice drummed in his head.

'Are you all right, my dear?' asked Dona Mónica as Xissola joined them again. She nodded.

'Look, here they come,' cried Chimene, excitedly. They all ran to meet Hadjame and her Grandma. Wassi greeted Hadjame with a long and passionate embrace.

'Would you mind if I gave my daughter a hug, please?' Dona Mónica interrupted them, politely.

'Of course, Dona Mónica. Your daughter is all yours,' said Wassi with a smile. He gave her Grandmother a hug and handed her the flowers. Xissola, although she felt really jealous at the scene, had also missed her friend, and she ran over to give her a big hug. Everyone was happy, including Wassi, who even managed to forget that Xissola was there. Grandma's surgery had been a success, and Dona Mónica invited her mother to stay with them for a while so they could look after her better. Hadjame rode in Wassi's car with Xissola, and she talked to her friend excitedly about her plans with Wassi. Her friend seemed distant. Ready for a new page in her life with Wassi, Hadjame was keen to make up for her mistakes of the past. They finally arrived at home, and as always, Maria had prepared a special meal for the occasion. Hadjame and Grandma talked about their trip to South Africa and also shared some presents with their family and friends, Hadjame had bought a nice pair of shoes for Chimene, as she had asked, and a nice frangrance for everyone.

'You need to think about our trip to England now. It's quite soon,' Chimene said to her sister when they were eating supper together later.

'I've been thinking about that. I don't think there's anything to stop me now,' replied Hadjame, looking at her boyfriend affectionately. They all laughed except Xissola.

'Excuse me, I need to go to the bathroom,' said Xissola, getting up from the table.

'Are you sure everything's all right, Xissola?' asked Dona Mónica, concerned about Xissola's earlier state at the airport.

'I think I'm going to be sick, Auntie' Xissola replied and ran to the toilet, feeling desperate. Hadjame followed her. Her friend was vomiting and had gone very pale. Hadjame was worried, but she decided not to ask her anything just then. She helped her clean herself up and they went back to the dining room.

'You look very pale, Xi!' Chimene said, leaving her embarrassed.

'I'd say she looks like she's pregnant,' concluded Grandma, confidently, with her years of experience. Wassi coughed, choking slightly when he heard Grandma's words.

'Here, drink this glass of water, Wassi, and Xissola go and lie down in my room a bit,' Hadjame said to her friend, distracting her from her Grandmother's remark.

'Who is the father, Xissola?' provoked Chimene, laughing at her. Xissola ignored her, and went off to Hadjame's room to lie down.

'You can be really unpleasant sometimes, Chimene,' Hadjame hissed to her. Chimene nodded with an innocent look. That night, Xissola slept in her friend's house, and she told her that her period was late.

'So, you are pregnant?' Hadjame asked. Xissola was really scared of how her mother would react, as she had always been very strict and conservative. Hadjame, too, was inclined to feel it was better to wait until you were married, but at that moment she advised her friend not to worry.

'My mother is going to kill me', I'm so scared, cried Xissola.

'Keep calm, let's talk to my mum first, she will help us,' suggested Hadjame. They both cried, and agreed to get a kit from the pharmacy the next day before talking with Hadjame's mother, who was more open-minded. Xissola cried a river almost all night, until falling asleep.

Early the next morning, the two friends returned from the shops with a test kit from the pharmacy. Without telling anyone, especially Grandma, who was sitting in the lounge watching TV, the two girls passed her quietly and went up to the bathroom.

'Well, Xissola?' Hadjame whispered from outside the door.

'It's positive,' said Xissola, crying as she opened the door. 'Now what am I going to do? My mother's going to kill me.'

'Shhhhh, stop crying.'

'Is everything all right, Hadjame?', Gradma asked. Hadjame had never felt such a great responsibility on her shoulders, but she could not abandon her friend at a time like this.

'Yes Grandma, everything's fine. 'Keep calm, Xi. Who's the father?' Hadjame asked. Xissola just went on crying, and crying, saying nothing. Hadjame decided not to press her and wait for a calmer moment. The two girls hugged each other and cried softly. Later on, Xissola left, her friend promising to do what she could to help her. Xissola decided to call Wassi, who did not want to hear from her at all.

'Wassi, answer me please, it's urgent,' Xissola left a third voice message for her friend, choking back the tears. Really alarmed when he listened to the messages, Wassi rushed off to meet her, and in a few hours Xissola heard Wassi knocking at her door.

'I have a lunch meeting between Hadjame and my father in half an hour. I hope this isn't another of your tricks,' he warned her, as she opened the door, and invited him in.

'It's not a trick at all. I'm pregnant, Wassi,' she confessed without wasting time. 'I'm nearly a month pregnant. I hadn't been with anyone for more than three months before that night we had dinner together.' Wassi listened to her in silence, not understanding.

'So?' he asked seriously, suspicious about where the conversation was heading.

"What do you mean, "So?" She could not manage to face him. Calmly, Wassi stood up for a few moments, trying to process the information.

' Are you saying that...You have to be joking,' he said at last.

'I'm not joking. My mother already knows all about it, and she wants to talk to you and your father on Saturday,' she said, her eyes full of tears.

'This has got to be a nightmare. What did you do that night?' Wassi asked her furiously. Xissola had never seen him like this. His eyes were expressionless and he shook her roughly, seeming to have lost his mind.

'I put a sleeping pill in your drink,' Xissola confessed fearfully, looking at the floor, then stopped, scared he would hit her. Silence filled the room. Wassi almost lost his head again, but he contained himself, and without saying a word, he turned and headed for the door.

'Wassi, wait please! Promise you'll come to my house on Saturday with your father, please,' she begged him, he listened to her in silence.

'Get out of my sight,' he yelled, so loud that Xissola almost fell down in shock. Wassi started the car roughly, totally out of control. In tears, Xissola knew he would come on Saturday, she then decided to ring Hadjame and ask her to come to her house on Saturday afternoon as well.

'But please don't tell anyone. Not even Wassi,' Xissola asked her friend.

'Don't worry, everything will be all right. You can count on me,' Hadjame said, trying to console her. The two friends said goodbye, and moments later Wassi arrived at his girlfriend's house.

'Sorry I'm late; something came up,' Wassi apologised to Hadjame, trying to stay calm. But he was sweating with agitation.

'I was beginning to think you weren't coming. You're

very tense. Is something the matter?' Hadjame asked him when they hugged. 'Do you still want to take me to see your dad?'

'Of course, and I'm sure he's going to be delighted to meet you in person,' said Wassi with a wan smile.

'It'll all be fine, relax,' she said innocently. They went off to Wassi's house. He tried to tell her the truth on the way, but he didn't have the courage, especially on a special day like this. In Wassi's house, Hadjame met his father, Senhor Marcos, who thought she was lovely. It was a very masculine apartment. It was obvious that there was no woman there to deal with the basics. Things were all over the place, but even so it felt very cosy.

'My son's made a good choice,' he said. Hadjame, embarrassed, smiled and thanked him. They talked a lot about her family, and Hadjame was pleased to learn that he had been operated on by her father in the past. The two men were quite different. Young in spirit and good-humoured, unlike her rather dictatorial father, Wassi's father told her a few amusing stories about himself and his son. But Wassi seemed very pensive, almost as though he was not aware of what was going on around him.

'Is everything all right, son?'

'Yes, fine, Dad,' he said, smiling timidly.

'You've hardly said a word,' said Hadjame. She and Senhor Marcos looked at each other and laughed at

Wassi's nervousness. He was acting like a teenager. In no time at all, Hadjame and Senhor Marcos were good friends. When lunch was over, Hadjame said goodbye to Wassi's father and thanked him for making her feel so welcome.

'Your father was really nice,' Hadjame said to Wassi. They chatted as he took her home.

'Thank you for coming,' said Wassi, as he parked the car in front of Hadjame's building. 'See you tomorrow.' He gave her a cool kiss. Hadjame went up to the flat, feeling concerned.

'So how did lunch with "Father-in-law" go?' Chimene asked, bursting with curiosity.

'Lunch was lovely, his father is lovely, but I'm a bit worried about Wassi. He didn't seem all right to me,' said Hadjame pensively. That evening, Hadjame shut herself up in her room, and then spent the night lying awake. Her thoughts kept turning to Wassi, when she wasn't trying to figure out a solution to her friend's problem for Saturday.

13
A Sudden Change

Hadjame guessed from the look on Auntie Sofia's face that she already knew the truth, and she felt the tension in the air as she was invited into her friend's house. Sitting down timidly, Hadjame felt as though she was sitting in the dock. But before she could even frame a question, the bell rang and Xissola's mother went to open the door. Hadjame got to her feet in alarm; she couldn't figure out what Wassi and his father were doing at Xissola's house.

'What are you, and your father doing here?' she asked Wassi.

'Calm down Hadjame', requested Xissola's mother, and invinted them all to sit down. Wassi sat down without answering her. Hadjame looked at everyone, half lost, waiting for an explanation.

'Hadjame, please sit down,' Xissola's mother requested again, making her even more nervous. Xissola didn't seem to know what to say, and Wassi, without the courage to face Hadjame, stared at the floor. His father's hand was on his shoulder to give him support. 'Xissola can tell you all about it now,' said her mother.

'Tell me what?' interrupted Hadjame. 'What's going on, Xi?'

'Please forgive me, Hadjame,' Xissola said at last. Kneeling in front of her, Xissola begged Hadjame forgiveness. Hadjame felt as though she was in the middle of a nightmare, and she wanted to wake up.

'Xissola, who is the father?' Hadjame asked, beginning to put the pieces together. Losing control, she stood up and looked at her friend, kneeling at her feet and at her boyfriend who could not manage to raise his head, soaking the floor with his tears. It all became clear, Wassi was the father of Xissola's child.

'Please forgive me, my dearest friend,' Xissola begged her, still on her knees, dragging herself towards her.

'Don't call me your friend. Get away from me, you traitor,' said Hadjame, furious. Yanking the pendant from her neck, she threw it in her friend's face.

'And as for you,' she said, turning to her boyfriend with her eyes full of tears, 'how could you?' Wassi did not say a word. He just cried. Feeling herself an intruder on this scene, Hadjame ran out of the house, distraught. The room was filled with silence, until Xissolas's mother gained the courage to speak.

'As you might already know, my daughter is nearly a month pregnant from your son,' she said to Wassi's father and he nodded. Wassi and Xissola both kept silent. 'For this reason, before the pregnancy gets bigger, we'd better marry them,' she said without beating around the bush. Wassi couldn't believe what his ears had just heard, he wanted to leave, he said he was not going to marry her, and he was not the father of Xissola's son. His fathet asked him to calm down.

'You can't shirk your responsibilities my son,' his father said, and Wassi sat down again, very upset. As they continued their conversation, both families agreed that the earlier the marriage, the better. Wassi couldn't believe what he had just got himself into.

As for Hadjame, she could not get her head around the fact that she'd lost her boyfriend to her best friend. Back home, Hadjame cried bitterly, regretting that she hadn't listened to her sister Chimene's warnings, she shut herself in her room and didn't eat for several days, causing her family a great deal of worry. Wassi called at the house to speak to her, but she refused to see him. He told her mother the truth, and Dona Mónica blamed herself for having placed her trust in Wassi without her husband's consent. Wassi apologised, saying he was really sorry and that it was an accident. There was nothing Dona Mónica could do but lament her daughter's suffering. Wassi left a note with Chimene, asking her to give it to Hadjame. But Hadjame just threw the note in the paper bin in her room without reading it, Maria kept it saved. Hadjame began to lose interest in the things she used to like doing. She didn't answer phone calls from either Xissola or Wassi, and cancelled her registration at the university.

'But, Hadjame, how can you cancel university before you've even begun?' her mother asked.

'For that very reason, Mum. I can't face beginning, at least for now,' she said to her mother. Hadjame could not forgive her friend and boyfriend, and things got even worse for her after their wedding. Hadjame felt as though the whole world was falling in around her, but she didn't want to believe that all this was happening to her. The wedding of Wassi and Xissola took place in a very simple ceremony, with few guests. Immediately afterwards, Wassi had to go back to England to continue his studies. Hadjame wept in her room day and night from all the pain this caused her until she decided to face the world again, and she turned into a rebellious girl. She seemed to be against everything and everyone.

The family trip to England was postponed due to her depressed state. Her mother even arranged a consultation with a psychologist to see if it would help, but Hadjame said she wasn't mad and didn't need to be seen by a psychologist. She got mixed up with some bad company, and started coming home late, and sometimes drunk. Her Grandma wept and wailed about her granddaughter's attitude. Whenever he rang, her father always argued with her mother, although Dona Mónica didn't know how to tell her husband the real reason for delaying her trip. Chimene felt very discontented because all the attention was on Hadjame, and the two girls argued incessantly.

'Do you think they give a stuff about you?' Chimene

asked when Hadjame was crying with disappointment. 'They are both married now, and there is nothing else that you can do.'

'Get out of my room, Chimene,' shouted Hadjame in fury. From her room, Grandma listened to her granddaughters arguing yet again.

'Dad's really worried, and Mum hasn't the courage to tell him that their "little princess" is depressed, and that's why we've had to put off our trip,' said Chimene. They went on arguing, until they heard Maria shouting in alarm. Their Grandma had been taken ill. They ran to her room.

'Grandma, what is it?' The girls asked.

'Maria, call an ambulance','Hadjame cried desperately. Grandma was lying unconscious on the floor, and the sisters hugged each other in tears when they saw their Grandma being taken off to hospital. Later on, their father learned all about what had been happening through Kizua, who spoke to Grandma. Although she was still in hospital, she told her grandson all about the bad feelings that had taken over the house.

'Why didn't you come to England when I asked you to? Things might well have taken a different course,' said their father, as he argued with their mother over the phone once more.

'You never paid much attention to our children. You've always been more interested in your work,' said their mother in her defence.

'And what a great contribution you've made, letting our daughter cancel her university course and take drugs,' said their father in a fury. They were on the verge of separating, and Chimene blamed her sister for everything that was happening in the family.

'I'm sorry. I didn't want to destroy our family. You should have gone to England,' said Hadjame to her mother and sister, in tears, blaming herself for everything.

'It's too late now. With Grandma in hospital, we won't be able to go, never,' said Chimene, annoyed. Finding herself guilty, Hadjame started to face reality again and her main concern now was over her Grandmother who was still in hospital.

'I'm so sorry Grandma, I promise to behave myself this time,' said Hadjame, and she hugged her Grandma who cried tears of sadness. The whole family visited Grandma in hospital every day. The doctor said it would be better for her to stay there for a while. Just as everything seemed to have calmed down, one night the family received a phone call from the clinic. They all rushed to the hospital, alarmed.

'We did everything we could, but we're sorry to tell you that we were unable to save her,' the doctor told the family. Unable to bear the shock, Dona Mónica collapsed, and Hadjame and Chimene were very desperate and they both cried in deep pain. Dona Mónica woke up in a hospital bed where, seeing the state of her daughters who sat at her bedside, she knew straight away that it had not been a nightmare. Minutes later, Chimene rang her father, and brother from the hospital to tell them about Grandma's death. Her father told them to stay calm and they should delay the funeral until he and Kizua returned. Kizua was shocked by the news, and he did not stop crying until they flew back to Luanda. In spite of her advanced state of pregnancy, Xissola turned up, too. She was welcomed by the whole family like the daughter she had always been to them.

'Go and give your friend some support; she needs it. You were always such good friends, and you have to forget what has happened in the past,' said Dona Mónica to Xissola. Hadjame was weeping miserably, alone in a corner, blaming herself for her Grandmother's death. Xissola approached her friend warily. Hadjame fell into her arms, and the two girls wept like children. Wassi rang the family from England to send his condolences, but Hadjame didn't want to hear him. She agreed only to speak to Marta and Bonitão, who rang from the US. After the funeral, Xissola disappeared again. She moved to another city and the only news they heard was that she has given birth to a lovely baby boy, who was strong and healthy, and named after his father, 'Junior'. Hadjame then decided to look to her own life again. She extricated herself from the company she'd been keeping, feeling they were leading her astray, and she agreed to consult a psychologist and accept treatment. Her parents were reconciled, and finally her mother and sister, travelled to England, except for her, who was adamant that she didn't want to see Wassi never again. She went to live with her brother Kizua, who had returned to Angola to work after completing his training, giving the lie to Grandma's words, when she had said that her grandson would never come back from England. Hadjame began her university course in psychology, and she kept in constant touch with the family by telephone. Devoting herself one hundred per cent to her education, she spared no thoughts for anything else. She even got to know a few young men at university, but lost interest in them very quickly, much to the concern of her family.

14
The Journey

Five years later

At home with the family, Hadjame was celebrating her success in gaining a Master's degree in Psychology. Following in the footsteps of her father and brother, Hadjame was now part of the family tradition of becoming doctors. Chimene, in contrast, was pursuing a career in journalism.

'Congratulations my daughter, you deserve every success,' her father said, toasting her. 'I have a surprise for you.' They all waited anxiously as their father handed his daughter a small gift-wrapped box. Hadjame opened it carefully, with no idea what it might be.

'It's a key?' she exclaimed, puzzled.

'To your new car,' said her father, proud of his 25-year-old daughter.

'Oh, Dad! Thank you so much,' said Hadjame, really pleased.

'And there's something else,' her father went on. 'A scholarship to the United States, where you will be among the finest psychologists in the world, studying for your doctorate.' Hadjame was so overcome, she hugged her father with tears in her eyes and thanked him again, and they all applauded.

'I'll want a new car too, when I'm 25,' muttered Chimene, feeling jealous.

'Of course, you'll have one too, my dear, but first of all, you need to be nice.' They all laughed. Then everyone toasted Hadjame's success again.

'Now all you need to do is to find a partner,' said her mother, who had talked of nothing else recently.

'What about your oldest child?' said Hadjame in her defence, pointing at Kizua. 'I come after him,' she joked.

'I'm not planning to marry any time soon, little sister,' said Kizua. At 28, he was only interested in going out with every young woman he met.

'Perhaps you'll meet someone interesting in the US,' said Chimene, who also never brought any young men home to meet the family. Hadjame suddenly felt sad, as she thought about how proud Grandma would have been at that moment. She had not heard from Xissola since the previous year, when a mutual friend had told her she was doing great with her education in another city. As for Wassi, he remained in the UK, thinking there was no point to going back to Angola. In her room, packing up her things for her trip, Hadjame unexpectedly came across a sealed envelope.

'Wassi?' she exclaimed, very surprised, remembering the day when Wassi had left the note in her house. She sat down on the bed and read the note, anxiously. 'You will have my heart, wherever I may be. Hadjame and Wassi, in love forever,' the note said. And the ghosts of the past were back with her again. With tears in her eyes, and good memories from the past of happy times at her lover's side, of Xissola and her Grandma who was no longer with them, she cried out in despair, wishing she could turn back the clock, and kept the note safely inside of her diary. In the night, because of the difference in time zones, Hadjame rang Marta to let her know that she would soon be coming to the United States. Marta was delighted, and invited her to come and live with her, and she agreed. Hadjame counted the days and hours until her trip. She believed that only this way would she be able to get away from all her ghosts, and soon Hadjame found herself on her way to the airport, 'the road to happiness' as she had got into the habit of calling this longed-for journey.

'We're all so proud to see you like this, so happy and fulfilled,' said her mother, seeing her off at the airport. When she heard the word 'happy,'' Hadjame knew that was not what she really felt, and she kissed goodbye to all her family. Then the prayer was said, the plane took off, and it seemed as though it had all been left behind. 'A great love vanishes, but hope prevails,' she thought sadly, writing in her diary on the plane. After a flight of several hours, Hadjame arrived on American soil, where she was met by Marta with a big hug.

'Welcome to US; I've missed you so much, my dear friend,' said Marta.

'I've missed you too. And Bonitão?' asked Hadjame, looking for her old friend, eager to see him again.

'He stayed in the apartment. He's making you a special lunch,' said Marta with delight.

'How romantic,' exclaimed Hadjame. They both laughed, and she went off with her friend to take a taxi to Marta's apartment. Hadjame complained about the cold, in spite of being wrapped up well. It was winter, and although it wasn't snowing anymore, there was still melting snow on the ground, which made the weather even colder. It took half an hour to get to the apartment, which was in a modern building, about ten storeys high. The driver parked in front of the building and helped her with her bags. The two young women took the bags up to the third floor in the elevator.

'Welcome to my little place, which is going to be yours, too, now,' said Marta, opening the door. There were lots of attractive pictures scattered around the house, and scale models of elegant buildings in one corner reflected her career as an architect. A good smell came from the kitchen, followed by Bonitão, who greeted Hadjame with a huge hug.

'My favourite new girl!' he said, remembering their times at high school. They embraced affectionately. 'You look really nice,' said Bonitão, who did think she was a bit thin after all she'd been through, but even so, Hadjame was still very pretty.

'You both seem happy, too. Is there something I don't know about?' she asked, waiting for the answer, concerning the engagement ring that Marta was wearing, Bonitão nodded, and Marta called her to come and see her room and put her luggage there. Hadjame got the message. The room was the perfect size, and very light, with enormous windows looking out over the pretty garden with its pond, where there were ducklings swimming about. The peace and quiet of the place made her forget all about the rest of what was out out there. Hadjame loved the room.

'Do you like it?' Marta asked. Hadjame was still looking outside. She nodded. 'I knew you would. That's why I decided to move to the other room.'

'Oh, Marta! You didn't have to do that,' said Hadjame, touched.

'That's what friends are for,' Marta replied. Hadjame hugged her friend and told her a little about her life, and later Marta left her to settle in. After unpacking her cases and taking a bath, Hadjame joined them at the table.

'So, are you going to tell me your secret now?' Hadjame, asked, looking at her two friends.

'Bonitão and I are engaged,' Marta burst out, showing her diamond ring, and clapping her hands in delight. She looked as though she were about to fall off her chair. Although it was good news, Hadjame felt sad and left behind. Everyone was happy except for her. Bonitão and Marta had met each other at the same time as she and Wassi had, and now they were one step away from marriage. She felt a pain in her chest, but these were her friends and so she had to share their happiness.

'So when's the wedding?' she decided to ask.

'Probably in nine months time. We're going to get married in Angola, with all the family around us,' explained Bonitão.

'That means I'll be able to come,' said Hadjame, who would be on summer holiday then. Hadjame proposed a toast to her friends. While they talked about all kinds of things, Hadjame spoke only of her aims and her education.

'I hope you like it,' said Bonitão modestly, talking about the meal he'd prepared.

'Everyone likes food that's made with so much love,' said Hadjame. 'It's just I don't want to put on weight.' Bonitão looked at her in astonishment. Even with the obsession with weight of twenty-first-century women, Hadjame was a fine example.

'Is there a man in your life, Hadjame?' asked Marta, getting straight to the point.

'You sound just like my mother,' she said, smiling. Marta and Bonitão threw each other a questioning look.

'And is there something wrong with not having someone?' asked Hadjame, feeling uncomfortable. Marta shook her head, but looking into her eyes, she could discern a certain sadness. They continued having their meal as the conversation flowed easily. After dessert and tea, they chatted for a while, and then Hadjame, tired after her long journey, went off to her room earlier to rest. She tried to shake off the feelings of jealousy she had for her friends. In spite of living in different apartments, they seemed really happy, and Bonitão was very affectionate and attentive to Marta. Suddenly she wanted to have a man in her life, but her heart was very closed to loving anyone. Only Wassi seemed to fit, and it was he who came into her mind as she lay there drifting off to sleep.

On the Monday morning, her alarm went off at half past seven. And at nine o'clock, after breakfast, Hadjame went off to the university to start finding her way around. In recent times only her studies kept her mind occupied and, standing in the long queue for the registration of new students, she recalled the canteen at the boarding school, and Wassi. She gave a wry smile, thinking of the coincidences in life, but then she felt sad again because it seemed that wherever she was, Wassi was in her thoughts, and that brought to mind again her friends' wedding.

'Are you OK?' asked a voice behind her.

'Yes, I'm fine,' replied Hadjame, startled. She had been lost in her thoughts and didn't even realise it was her turn in the queue. She looked at the young man. He was just the type that Chimene was so keen to meet: tall, with blue eyes and blond hair. She thanked him and went to register. Later, she greeted the young man again, who was appraising her with a friendly smile. Back at home, she told her friend about her day. Marta told her off for not paying any attention to the other young men around her. Feeling dejected, Hadjame confessed that she had never forgotten Wassi and that she couldn't get him out of her mind. She thought that perhaps it was because it was an unresolved romance, and that just when she had thought everything was going to go well, she had lost him forever, and that was why she never got over it. Now the ghosts of an unresolved past, an unfinished romance, would pursue her forever, wherever she went.

'I'll do everything I can to help you,' Marta said, to console her. Forgetting her personal problems, Hadjame chatted to her friend about the wedding, wanting to know what they were planning, how many guests they would have, and what Marta's dress was going to be like. Marta seemed so excited about her wedding day. They both truly loved each other.

15
They Meet Again

January was always a time with lots of snow. That Saturday, no one dared go out into the street. Hadjame was reading her university notes in her room. She loved her psychology course and soon she was going to be able to use the title 'Doctor'. 'Doctor and unhappy', she thought sorrowfully, whenever she reread Wassi's note. 'Hadjame and Wassi in love forever,' she repeated with a smile. She was startled when Marta suddenly appeared in front of her, where she could see the note Hadjame was reading.

'I didn't hear you come in,' she said, embarrassed, and stuck the note between two books.

'You still love that man, don't you?' Marta said, and suddenly she was interrupted by a mysterious phone call, in which she seemed to be talking to Bonitão about someone's arriving.

'Who's arriving today, if you don't mind me asking?' Hadjame asked, her curiosity aroused.

'Just a package. By the way, Bonitão and I are eating out

this evening,' Marta said, changing the subject. Hadjame suspected that her friend was hiding something, as she seemed to be avoiding her eyes.

'Is everything all right, Marta?' she insisted.

'Of course,' Marta replied, still avoiding her eye. Hadjame nodded and continued reading her university notes. At seven in the evening, Bonitão called to pick Marta up.

'I don't know how you do it. It's damned freezing out there,' said Hadjame. 'Have fun!' She waved them off, and they went off to a restaurant, after they left, she felt a great solitude in the cold apartment. She decided to do a bit more work to keep herself occupied. Then the doorbell rang.

'I suppose you forgot the key again,' she muttered as she opened the door.

'Wa…Wass…Wassi?' she stammered, looking as though she had seen a ghost. Disconcerted, Hadjame tried to hide the note that was in her hand, but it fell to the floor. Wassi smiled when he recognised the note, and he picked it up. Lost for words, Hadjame snatched it from his hands.

'That note still holds true today, princess,' he said with an innocent smile. Hadjame was so embarassed, and that moment was thinking she would gladly have strangled Marta. Suddenly the world stopped turning. That male figure in front of her excited all her senses, and even before she could say anything, Wassi pulled her to him, and without saying anything, although her mind told her to get away. Hadjame let herself be consumed; she was easy prey. The only sounds were their moans of pleasure. Wassi gently kissed her all over, and with tears in her eyes, she asked him breathlessly to love her.

'Are you going to stay there, or are you going to invite me in?' he asked with the air of a gallant suitor.

'I'm.. I'm so sorry. Please come in,' she said, embarrassed. Wearing a dark winter coat and a blue scarf, Wassi looked like a French film actor. 'Have a seat and I'll be right back.' Hadjame rushed off to check herself in the mirror, feeling terribly nervous. 'You'll pay for this, Marta,' she said, cursing her friend, and returned to the lounge to attend to her unexpected guest, trying to look relaxed.

'Why didn't you tell me you were coming?' she asked, sitting down some distance away from him.

'Because then it wouldn't have been a surprise,' he replied, at ease. He took off his coat, laid it down delicately, and came to sit down next to her. Hadjame breathed in his perfume.

'And are you going to tell me why you've come?' she asked, shifting herself away, towards the edge of the sofa.

'I've missed you, I wanted to see you again…as friends, of course,' he said. Cautiously he moved nearer to her. 'Is that a problem?' he asked her.

'Of course not,' Hadjame said, getting up. The word

‘friends’ sounded strange to her ears, and there were tears in her eyes.

‘You still looking very nice. Are you crying?’ asked Wassi, standing up as well. He wanted to embrace her, but decided not to take the risk.

‘Yes, I’m crying, happy now? Who do you think you are, coming here and invading my life after everything you have done?’ she burst out, releasing all the grief that she carried in her chest. Wassi was bewildered and didn’t know what to say.

‘We still have to talk. Would you like to go somewhere else to talk? There’s a nice place near here,’ he suggested tactically. Hadjame remembered their walk on the beach together, at the boarding school. Everything seemed to go back in time, only it was different now.

‘I can’t. I have a date.’ She said for Wassi’s surprise.

‘Who with, if you don’t mind telling me?’

‘Derek,’ she lied. ‘If there was a Derek somewhere in the world, I, too, wouldn’t mind knowing him, she thought.

‘Derek’s a very lucky man,’ said Wassi sadly. Hadjame nodded. ‘I promise I won’t take up much of your time,’ said Wassi in a concerned voice. Hadjame didn’t know whether to cry or smile at the scene she had just created. Wassi thought that Derek really was someone in her life.

‘Would you like a pizza?’ she asked. Confused and

looking at his watch, Wassi thought Derek might turn up at any moment, but he accepted gladly.

'Thank you for this bit of time,' he said gratefully.

'I didn't know anything. No one told me anything.'

'I know, but I'm grateful just the same,' he replied, following her into the kitchen. Wassi picked up glasses for a drink while she put the pizza in the oven. They went back into the lounge and talked in a slightly more relaxed way, although Wassi kept looking at his watch. Hadjame smiled, and inside she felt so much happiness at seeing him again.

'A toast to our meeting again,' he said, smiling and handing her a glass of wine. He approached her and touched her lips gently and they both kissed each other desperately, as though they had been waiting for that kiss all their lives. Suddenly the two were interrupted by the fire detector and ran to shut it off. They could not stop laughing at their distraction. The pizza was thrown into the bin and replaced by another. This time they decided to stay in the kitchen to keep an eye on it. While they ate their pizza, they made a toast, looking into each other's eyes.

'So, tell me why you never rang me, and never answered my calls?' Wassi asked concerned.

'Because there was no more need,' she replied coldly.

'You never really believed in me, did you?'

'Believing in something so obvious is pretty difficult,

don't you think?' she said frankly, taking a gulp of her wine.

'But you know I always loved you, in spite of it all. I have a son, I know, but I am single.'

'How so, single?' asked Hadjame, smiling at the irony. 'Being apart doesn't make things any different.'

'I'm not joking. There's never been anything between Xissola and me, either before or after the marriage,' Wassi smiled, at ease.

'You two had a child, and you tell me that there was never anything?' Wassi shook his head.

'Not as far as I can remember. And as for my son, I pay his allowance. I know it may seem insensitive, but I'm planning to do a DNA test on my son when I get back.'

'Can I see a photo of him?' Hadjame interrupted him with a bit of curiosity and he took a picture from his wallet and showed it to her.

'His name is Junior, he is six years old now,' he said, a bit proudly, and she nodded. She saw Junior for the first time, and she smiled as she looked carefully at him. He was a very handsome and smart babe and looked just like Xissola, but it was not Junior's fault that Hadjame felt so uncomfortable. She gave Wassi back the photography.

'So, why did you marry her?' she asked, trying to hold back her tears.

'Because that's what her mother wanted.'

'This is like being in a play,' she said, not convinced. Wassi knelt at her feet. Very serious and with tears in his eyes, he declared all his love for her.

'I just can't stop myself from loving you. It's stronger than I am,' he said with his eyes full of tears, down on his knees.

'It's all so confusing for me. I never could reconcile myself with what happened, and I have no intention now of getting involved with a married man. Married to my best friend! That's not what I wanted for myself,' she wailed. Wassi begged her forgiveness and she felt very touched and could really see truth in his eyes. They kissed each other passionately again, and then they said goodbye, both in tears. Hadjame asked him not to ring her too soon because she still felt very confused. He tried to convince her to the contrary, but she was very determined in her decision. Wassi left, devastated. Alone in the flat again, Hadjame thought about Wassi and all he had just told her. She waited for Marta to come home, and when she heard the door open, Hadjame rushed out of her room like a wild thing.

'You traitor,' she said, clutching a slipper in her hand.

'Calm down, Hadjame. What's the matter?' asked Marta with an air of innocence, dodging away from her friend. The two of them ran around the flat.

'Don't pretend, Marta. I'm talking about Wassi.'

'Chimene tried to tell you, but I wouldn't let her,' said Marta, angering her friend still further.

'Even Chimene knew? All three of you will pay for this,' said Hadjame, standing on top of the sofa, trying to block Marta's way.

'But you were pleased, weren't you?' said Marta, provocatively. She ran to her room and managed to escape the slipper, which hit her door.

'You had no right,' shouted Hadjame.

'You still love him very much; I can see it in your eyes. That's why we had to do something,' said her friend, peeping out.

'I don't know. All I know is that it's very confusing.' Hadjame seemed to have calmed down a bit, and Marta approached her.

'But he isn't with Xissola. He told us that every time he came from London to visit us. You love each other; you should be together.'

'He's still married, and after everything that's happened I don't know if I can do it, this is so wrong,' said Hadjame sadly. 'But you can't imagine the fright I got.' They both laughed uncontrollably as Hadjame told her friend all about it, including the phantom boyfriend 'Derek,' which made Marta laugh even louder until her ribs hurt. And finally she told her about the passionate kiss. Marta listened to her like someone watching a romantic movie. Later on, they said goodnight and went to bed. Hadjame wanted to hear Wassi's voice, but she knew that he would not ring her so soon, respecting her wishes.

The next day, Hadjame woke up feeling really happy, and even lost her appetite, just drinking a glass of juice before setting off to the university.

'Today I am very happy. I feel as though something good is about to happen. Perhaps it's your wedding, since nothing of the sort is happening to me,' she said to Marta. And they both laughed and talked about the wedding, which was getting very close.

16
The Wedding

The long-awaited moment had arrived. The wedding preparations were steaming ahead. It was going to be a big event. Although Hadjame felt incomplete, and not very lucky in love, Marta and Bonitão were very happy and that was what mattered. In Marta's house there was such bustle it reminded her of the school dances. Like any bride, Marta was very anxious and nervous and her friend tried to boost her courage.

'I don't know what I'd do without you, my favourite psychologist,' Marta teased her.

'That's what friends are for,' replied Hadjame, who was helping Marta and her maid of honour get ready. Bonitão was getting ready in his apartment and they would only see each other at the registry office. Marta's parents were taking care of the reception, which was going to be held in the beautiful garden of their house. The two friends were amused to watch the behaviour of the couple through the window, going incessantly around and around, issuing instructions to ensure everything was perfect.

'My mother's such a perfectionist. My poor old dad, having to be out there helping her!' said Marta and they both laughed. 'It's certainly all going to be perfect, but it's a shame that you and Wassi aren't going to be best man and maid of honour.' Hadjame was saddened by this unexpected remark.

'That's not my fault!' She replied defensively, although feeling a bit sad.

'Don't worry, my dear, your day will come too,' the maid of honour encouraged her.

'Tell me the date and time, please, because I need to know,' Hadjame joked, 'If it doesn't happen soon, Chimene will be getting married before me,' and they all laugh.

'Hadjame, your mobile is ringing,' the maid of honour called to her.

'Could you answer it for me please, Ana?' asked Hadjame, unable to come while she was making the final adjustments to her friend's dress. 'Who is it?'

'Someone called Wassi,' replied Ana. When she heard Wassi's name after such a long time, Hadjame's heart began to beat faster.

'Tell him I'm really busy,' she said, acting uninterested.

'It doesn't help trying to avoid him. He'll be at the reception later,' Marta reminded her.

'He seems very distressed,' said the maid of honour.

Convinced, Hadjame took the phone from Ana's hands abruptly.

'Hello…Wassi,' she answered at last. There was silence at the end of the line. 'Wassi, are you there?'

'Yes, I'm here,' he said quietly, as if it was breaking the promise. 'Hadjame. I just rang to tell you about Xissola,' he continued.

'How come? What about her?' asked Hadjame worried.

'She had been in hospital for over two months, and she really wants to see you.' Hadjame went pale, and found herself unable to speak. When she saw her friend's reaction, Marta took the phone from her and finished the conversation with Wassi, who told her what was happening.

'I'm going over there right now,' said Hadjame, gathering up her things. Marta wanted to go with her, but Hadjame told her to stay. It was her wedding day, after all, and Xissola would certainly not be pleased.

'Don't forget to let us know,' Marta said.

'I won't,' said Hadjame, setting off hurriedly for the hospital. When she saw Wassi again, she felt a strong desire to embrace him, but did not dare have the courage, which actually made things easier. Like a child seeking protection, Wassi came to meet her and wept on her shoulder. Hadjame hugged him and could feel his heart beating.

'Where is she? Why did no one tell me?' she asked, remembering why she was there.

'I didn't know either. Her mother rang me not long ago. Apparently Xissola didn't want to say anything to anyone,' he told her. Minutes later, carrying Junior in her arms and looking very downcast, Xissola's mother came out of her daughter's room and said that Xissola was asking for both of them. Hadjame gave her a hug and kissed Junior on his face, and then she and Wassi went into the room. When she saw the state Xissola was in, Hadjame couldn't hold back the tears. Wassi, too, was very distressed, but he kept a little distant, as though scared to come too close. Hadjame slowly approached her friend's bed and took her hand. Xissola was freezing cold.

'I'll leave you alone now, but call us if there is an emergency,' said the nurse as she went out. Hadjame felt her chest tighten with a sense of guilt for having abandoned her friend for so long. Xissola was unrecognisable. She was very thin, her skin was covered with blemishes, and her lips were dry and sore. She no longer resembled anything like the lively and beautiful girl from six years ago.

'Hadjame, is it you?' she asked, semi-conscious.

'Shhhhhh, yes it's me, Xi, but don't make too much effort,' Hadjame whispered to her, squeezing her hand.

'My dear friend, how lovely that you have come. I've missed you so much,' said Xissola in a weak voice, with tears in her eyes.

'I've missed you, too. But you're going to get better and everything will all go back to how it was before,'

Hadjame said, to encourage her. Xissola started to cough, and kept having to stop and get her breath back before she could speak again.

'Please forgive me for everything.'

'Don't strain yourself. I forgive you.' Hadjame said, and Xissola gave her a wan smile. She smiled back.

'Do you remember when you said you would always have me in your heart?' Xissola asked.

'I do remember, and I do still have you in my heart.'

'I've always worn the necklace ever since the day you gave it back to me. But now you can take it; it's yours again.' Hadjame took the necklace from her friend's neck, and placed it on her own.

'Today is Marta and Bonitão's wedding day,' Hadjame said, trying to cheer her friend up by changing the subject.

'Is she happy?'

'They love each other very much. That's what matters.'

'And are you happy?' asked Xissola, looking her in the eyes. Hadjame said nothing and just gave her a smile. 'Hadjame, I'm afraid,' she continued.

'There's no need to be afraid. I'm going to squeeze your hand tightly, like we did when we were kids, do you remember?' Xissola nodded. 'I'm here with you, Xi.'

'I know. But there's something else that you both have

to promise me,' Xissola went on, beckoning Wassi to come closer. 'Promise me that you will look after Junior for me?'

'Junior is my son, I will always take care of him,' Wassi replied, slightly puzzled. Hadjame felt that her friend really was saying goodbye, and she did not want to accept it.

'You're going to be fine, and you will look after your son with…' She couldn't manage to say Wassi's name, it was all still too much for her.

'With Wassi, you mean,' Xissola finished her sentence. Hadjame nodded. 'I have to make a confession to you,' said Xissola, coughing hard and looking at Wassi. Hadjame listened to her attentively. 'That night we had dinner together, I put a sleeping pill in your drink because I wanted to seduce you, but nothing happened between us because you fell asleep straight away.' Astonished, Hadjame looked at Wassi, who drew nearer. 'I was already two weeks pregnant, before that night.'

'You are telling me that Ju…' Wassi tried, but couldn't finish.

'Yes, Wassi. Junior is not your child. I'm really sorry.' Wassi's eyes filled with fury. Hadjame stood there with her mouth open. She had never seen Wassi like that. And if it hadn't been for the state Xissola was in, he might well have lost his head. 'My mother would have killed me if I told her that I didn't know the father of my child, and as you were always fighting, I set this up to win you. She started to cough, again. 'Wassi loves you very much, Hadjame,' she continued. 'He never betrayed you with me, not even after we got married; instead, he decided to go to England. You have to be together.' She stopped to catch her breath. 'Only promise me you will look after Junior.' She continued.

'I promise to take care of Junior,' Hadjame replied, moved.

'And promise that you forgive me, too.'

'Yes, I forgive you,' said Hadjame, crying and hugging her friend. Angry, Wassi left without saying a word. Xissola took a turn for the worse when she saw his reaction. Hadjame called the nurse, scared. The doctor came and asked her to leave the room for a few minutes. Outside, in the waiting room, they all waited, hoping for good news. Several hours later, the doctor came over, and they all gathered around him.

'Doctor, how is she?' Xissola's mother asked impatiently.

'How is she Doctor?' Hadjame insisted.

'I'm really sorry, but…'

'But what, Doctor?' her mother asked. The doctor seemed unable to find the right words.

'We tried everything,' he said at last, shaking his head. Hadjame sat down on the floor. Wassi knelt down beside her and they hugged each other, crying. Xissola's mother fainted and a nurse tried to revive her. Junior looked on uncomprehending, then felt frightened and began to cry, calling for his Grandmother.

'It's my fault, Wassi,' said Hadjame, in tears. 'I want to see my friend for the last time.' She stood up, trying to release herself from Wassi's arms. He held her tightly.

'It's no one's fault, Hadjame. These things happen,' he said.

'I abandoned her all this time.'

'She didn't want to tell anyone,' Wassi reminded her.

'Another reason for me to be near when she needed me most. But anyway, what was wrong with her?' asked Hadjame, addressing Xissola's mother, who had now come round.

'Xissola was HIV positive,' confessed her mother, in great distress. 'She discovered it when she was pregnant, and that's why she distanced herself from everyone. She rejected the medication, and did not accept her condition. Luckily my grandson was not infected,' she said in tears. Junior seemed to have begun to grasp what was happening and he began to ask for his mother, crying.

'I'll take care of you, little one,' said Hadjame, picking him up, and he seemed to like her as he stopped crying. Everyone was very shocked. Hadjame rang Marta to tell her what had happened. Marta wanted to postpone the wedding, but Hadjame asked her to go ahead for Xissola's sake and for her mother, who would probably have a fit if her daughter put off the wedding after all the work that had gone into it. After much insistence, Marta agreed. The funeral was going to be in three days' time and then would be the time for mourning and grief. Wassi, Hadjame, and the whole family except for Chimene, who had been held up, could not miss the wedding. In a civil and religious ceremony, Pedro Manuel, also known as Bonitão and Marta exchanged wedding rings and were united. Everyone applauded as they kissed. At the reception, the couple were congratulated by everyone, who gathered round to wish them well again. None of them were happy, especially Marta, but she tried to live up to the moment as best she could.

'Don't be like that, Marta. Xi would certainly have been very happy to see you happy today,' said Hadjame as she congratulated her friend. Hadjame spotted Wassi far off, chatting to Kizua, and it was obvious that they were talking about her, which made her feel uncomfortable. Chimene arrived at the reception later, putting everybody in the shade with her chic outfit. She was in the company of an attractive Englishman whom nobody knew. She called her sister over to introduce him.

'Hadjame!' Wassi called her suddenly, as she was on her way to see Chimene. 'Will you marry me?' he asked her seriously, as though with no more time to lose. And everyone turned to her to see what she would say.

'What's this about, Wassi?' she asked, embarrassed. He went up to her and knelt down. Hadjame smiled, thinking it was a joke, and told him to get up and everyone applauded the romantic scene.

So, do you accept or not?' he insisted. Hadjame thought about Xissola's confession, and then realised how short life really was, and her heart burst with a mixture of so much sadness and happiness, but she didn't know what to say. 'Chimene gave her a nudge with her elbow to get her to say something.

'It's what I want most in the world,' she replied quietly. Wassi kissed her deeply and Hadjame wept as she remembered the death of her friend and all that had happened before she could live this moment with the one she loved.

'Congratulations to the newlyweds, and a toast to the newly engaged!' Kizua called out, embracing and congratulating his sister and friend. Then everyone came up to congratulate them.

'I didn't know your day would be exactly on the same day as mine, you stealer,' Marta whispered in her ear to congratulate her friend. Hadjame smiled timidly.

'No one said it'd be easy,' said Chimene as she approached her sister to congratulate her and introduce her new friend for the first time. 'Jack' was his name. Both sisters hugged each other. More than ever, Hadjame now understood the meaning of her old father's words. Finally Hadjame and Wassi were together again, and nothing was going to keep them apart this time around as their tight hug showed. She whispered in his ear a few words and Wassi heard her in silence.

'I will always carry you in my heart.' She held her silver heart-shaped pendant as she said it. Wassi knew those words were meant for Xissola.

About the Author

Suzeth Mawote was born in the north of Angola in 1983, but she grew up in the capital of Angola-Luanda, where she attended primary and secondary schools, and later on at a young age went to a boarding School at The National Institute of Petroleum in Sumbe Province. Since an early age, she had a pure passion for writing. She used to be a member of the "Union of Angolan writers" where she had met with some of the greatest writers of the Country and learnt more skills from them. Presently, she lives in Scotland where she is undertaking her university course in Geology and Petroleum Geology at the University of Aberdeen and "No-one said it'd be easy" is her debut novel.

www.ingramcontent.com/pod-product-compliance
Ingram Content Group UK Ltd.
Pitfield, Milton Keynes, MK11 3LW, UK
UKHW040015200726
13854UKWH00001B/222

9 781452 093291